HOW YOU GET THE GIRL

from the author of *Evergreen*

JESSICA FLORENCE

This is a work of fiction. Names, places, characters, and events are fictitious in every regard. Any similarities to actual events, and persons, living or dead, are purely coincidental. Any trademarks, service marks, product names, or named features are assumed to be the property of their respective owners, and are used only for reference. There is no implied endorsement if any of those terms are used. Except for review purposes, the reproduction of this book in whole or part, electronically or mechanically, constitutes a copyright violation.

Jessica Florence© **2017**

Editing by LibrumArtis Editorial Services

Proofreading by Judy's Proofreading

Cover by Sarah Hansen, Okay Creations©

This book is dedicated to Fun Love

The type of love that you can laugh, smile, and enjoy.

<3

Prologue

Joel Kline

"Hello, Lips." I was stunned by the woman that just walked into the bar: tanned skin, brown hair, legs for miles in that sweater dress, and swollen pink lips. The exact color of her light eyes were hard to tell in this dim light, but the whole package together made her look exotic, like a freaking Victoria's Secret model. When her eyes collided with mine then continued to peruse my body, I was already contemplating my approach. Then the pink on her cheeks showed up, and that was it. My feet were moving, and my eyes were holding hers. I could tell by the way she was looking at me that she knew what type of man I was— a man that would fuck her into the morning hours and still have her screaming for more.

She watched me as I placed myself in front of her and leaned in, my lips caressing the wispy tendrils of hair around her ear.

"I know you liked what you saw. Time to sign the deal. Let's go home." I pulled back and put on my special movie star smolder that always worked with the opposite sex. They liked to bag the title holder of the Sexiest Man Alive award, but the smolder was what made their panties drop.

I wasn't quite prepared for the surprisingly hard smack to my cheek, because to be honest, it's never happened before.The feeling was odd.

She looked at me with disgust, turning on her heels and swaying that sweet, apple bottom ass of hers away from me. Wishing my teeth were sinking into it instead, I sighed and returned to my best friend, Killian, who was sulking at the bar over woman problems.

"Have fun?" He had a smirk on his face, clearly finding my rejection funny.

"Chick's got spunk. Made my dick hard." It did, actually. I wasn't much of a man that mixed pain and pleasure, but I think with her fiery spirit I would be drawn to that type of kink. I grabbed a shot and downed it; the burn in my throat did nothing to ease the sting on my cheek. I watched her as she scanned the rest of the room, looking for who she wanted to play with tonight and coming up short. She was a man eater for sure, which kinda wanted to ruffle her feathers, so I'd get to see that wild in her come forward. An idea hit me, and I couldn't wait to see the look on her face.

"Be right back," I said to Killian, and walked over to the little DJ booth.

"Hey, that girl in the blue sweater dress said she really wanted to sing the next song, but was nervous. Will you take the choice out of her head?" I called out to the dread-headed DJ, and he gave me a thumbs-up. The person who was currently slaughtering their song was almost done, so I went back to Killian and waited for the moment to happen.

"What'd you do?" he asked, but then a bunch of girls latched onto me. Normally I would find this entertaining, but right now I didn't care; I wanted to see what my little spicy vixen would do when the DJ called her up.

When he did, and her eyes were throwing swords at me, I had to repress my belly laugh. This was priceless. She wasn't the type of woman to let things go. Honestly, I bet she would be the type to rip your pillows into shreds and then smash your windshield with a bat. A Harley Quinn-like woman.

Crazy, but fuck if it didn't turn me on.

She walked onto the stage, whispered to the DJ, and grabbed the mic. She was planning something devious, and it was making my dick twitch just watching her retaliate from my scheme.

"This song goes out to all you ladies who think you're leaving with a prime steak, but all you got is a hot dog." That voice. Dear sweet baby Jesus, did she have an accent? Fucking hell, she sounded so hot.

When she started singing Cowboy Casanova by Carrie Underwood, I was a goner. Not sure how in the world things were going to happen between us, but I felt our fates intertwine as she wiggled those hips, and told these women on my arms that I was a devil in disguise.

We watched her, and after she left the bar, I wasn't in the mood to be around people. I just wanted my home, my friend, and the Pacific beneath my board.

"Let's get out of here."

As we drove back to my home in La Jolla, I couldn't help but think if I knew any way or had contacts who could find that woman. I wasn't ready for this little story of ours to be over.

Chapter One

Alessandra

"I can do this." My words disappeared into the empty trailer as I looked over my new work station for the next four months. Everything was organized, all my makeup and special effects products were laid out for me to grab easily. I had been a makeup artist for close to ten years now; it was basically second nature to me.

So why was my heart beating erratically, and my palms starting to sweat a little? My eyes found themselves in the brightly lit mirror in front of me.

"Okay, you're going to be working on Joel Kline, all day, every day, for the next four months." I knew the answer to my own question. No use fighting myself like it was some great mystery.

Joel Kline was Hollywood's hottest actor. He was huge right now, especially after his last movie with the comic book studio. Everyone knew who he was, especially me. I watched my cheeks turn pink as I thought about the first time I met him.

He was at the bar, looking sexy as hell, just like he always does on screen. But this time he was flesh and blood, and I swore I could feel the heat from his gaze on me. I had been on the hunt for a man to play with for the night, but as soon as I saw him, I changed my mind. It had been a while since I had been with a guy, and I wasn't going to start with that one.

Nope. I wouldn't get involved with Joel Kline in any way if I could help it. He was too much. My body would love it; I saw that in his eyes. He promised a great night between us. But the damage to my life could be astronomical. Cameras followed him everywhere; some even came up online about that night the morning after. I looked! I couldn't play with that bonfire. Nope.

When he whispered his line to me, it all but sealed the deal. It was stupid. What woman would fall for that crap? He was good-looking, but dumb as a rock. I bet he couldn't have an actual conversation with someone without trying to use his looks to get whatever he wants. Now he had status to help him out even more.

I'll admit he is a pretty good actor. My son, Jenson, idolizes him right now, which is yet another reason not to get involved with him.

My son.

Shaking my head, I didn't wanna think about how much of a protective mama I was right now.

Checking my appearance once more, I decided I looked good, and professional. I was not about to wear cut-off shorts or anything that signaled to a man that I was up for grabs. He made it very clear he would fuck with me any chance he could.

I still can't believe he signed me up to sing on stage, but joke was on him. I was a feisty bitch. I looked him in the eye, and the girls that were hanging on him, and turned it back around.

"You are not going to let him rile you up," I told myself in the mirror.

I smacked my red lips at myself, and ran my sweaty hands over the thighs of my jeans. My black hair was rolled in a pinup-like style and my makeup was on point to show off my blue eyes and long lashes. My oversized but fashionable sweater looked cute with my skinny jeans tucked into my knee-high, flat boots. I was comfortable, yet functional. I didn't know how some of these women wore heels all day. I loved heels, but not when I was on my feet for hours, like I would be today. I looked at the clock on the desk in front of me. Almost 7:00 a.m. He should be here at any moment.

The door creaked open, and Lisa, the key makeup artist, along with Joel stepping into the trailer behind her.

Seeing him in person made me say a silent prayer to the heavens that he didn't remember me from the bar. It was over a month ago, so I mentally crossed my fingers.

Then his eyes met mine. Those piercing, light-blue-almost-silver eyes found mine, and his lips went up one side. He definitely remembered me. Oh well, there went that prayer.

"Alessandra! On top of the game, as usual." Lisa smiled at me then looked at Joel.

"Joel Kline, meet Alessandra Rose. Alessandra, meet Joel." She did a quick introduction for us, and then asked him to sit in the chair facing the mirror. We needed to go over everything one more time, with Joel present, so I could see his face properly.

He and I hadn't said anything to one another, but his eyes would meet mine in the mirror occasionally. I just ignored it.

When Lisa felt I was ready to fly on my own, she left the trailer to go check on the other artists.

"Tilt your head up, now to the right. Close your eyes," I directed him, keeping up the professionalism in the room. It wouldn't last long though; I knew he wouldn't stay quiet.

"I've imagined you so many times in my head since our first meeting." He approached the elephant in the room with that. I just rolled my eyes.

"I'm sure you have." He simply hummed hearing my voice. Maybe thinking about those probably dirty thoughts he's had before.

"Just as sexy as I remember, and feisty." This was going to be a long four months, if he kept this up. Time for me to lay down the law.

"Okay, open your eyes, and then look at me," I directed him. He did, and I was momentarily stuck looking into his eyes. They weren't hiding any of the lust and desire he held for me. It was a little unnerving.

"I am your new makeup artist for the next four months. I will not be sleeping with you, nor having any sort of relationship other than a professional one. And don't try to take that as a challenge, either. I've got too much riding on this to screw it up with you. So yes, we met before at a bar and you threw some stupid line at me. I smacked your pretty boy face because you deserved it. Then you tried to get me back by making me sing, which I did, and it felt good. That's it. There's no more to our story. Got it?" I pointed my brush at him, being completely serious. He just flashed his white teeth at me and didn't say a word for a few seconds, which was starting to rile me up on the inside a bit.

"I feel like there's more to our story, Lips."

Lips. I scoffed at his use of the word as a nickname for me.

"That's not an attractive nickname."

"You've got the sexiest lips I've ever seen."

"Okay, I think we are done here. Let's just finish your makeup so you can move onto wardrobe. You have a galaxy to save, and a princess to seduce." I tried to move on to better subjects, like finishing up my work so he could go make movie magic.

"Okay, Princess." His smile grew, if that was even possible, signaling that it was time I shut up and moved on. Anything I said could be used against me by this man. He stayed quiet for the remainder of our time and then a cute little blonde with a blue streak in her hair waltzed into his trailer. She popped a gum bubble as she walked over to us.

"Ready to get some sexy space warrior gear on?" She wore denim shorts and a button-up blue plaid shirt with black Doc Martins. I said hi to her earlier while grabbing breakfast in the parking lot, but she didn't acknowledge me.

"You know it." He stood and grabbed my hand before I could react, bringing it to his lips and pressing a kiss against my skin. A chill shot down my veins, but I wouldn't let him see that. He placed my hand back at my side, winked, then headed to the closet on the other side of the trailer to go over his clothes for the scenes today.

When my eyes found my face in the mirror, I knew I was in trouble. My cheeks were pink, and my eyes were lustful.

"One down, only three months and thirty days to go," I told the woman in the mirror.

Chapter Two

Joel

"Cut!" Leighton, our director, shouted. It was time for a break. We'd been shooting all day, and I was starving. But at least I didn't fuck up my lines, so we only did a few retakes here and there.

We had been shooting for about a week, and everything was going smoothly.

For the most part this story would feature just me, the lone warrior, battling his way across time and space to rescue the love of my life. A woman who picked up a book in which I was trapped. As she read my story, I would be getting closer and closer to her. Then in the end, I would almost die, if she didn't confess her love to me. A fictional character, in her eyes, but she still falls in love, regardless, thus freeing me from the book and into her life.

The movie was based on a bestselling book. People fell for the story, saying it was like The Never Ending Story, except for adults. When I auditioned for this role, I had read the book, and truly embodied the character, Luc. He was strong, cunning, and loved the owner of the book with all his being. Truly an interesting story.

I walked over to the catering table and jumped right in with a plate. Leighton came over to talk to me. I listened to what he said about shooting the scene we just did a different way, but when Alessandra walked by, everything the director said went in but never registered.

She was into me. I could tell by the blush on her cheeks, and the way her eyes lit up when we bantered. It was like foreplay, in a way, for us. Every time I had to get my makeup touched up, she would try to ignore me, and I would try to rile her up. She and I had been going back and forth with each other since that first day. Nothing extravagant—a little conversation here, a little wink there, and then she would roll her eyes, and shut down all my attempts to seduce her.

"Ten more minutes, then we go back in," Leighton said and then walked away. Wish I had heard more of what he'd said instead of entertaining myself by thinking about foreplay with Alessandra.

God, even her name was like foreplay to me. It sounded sexual, perfect for the temptress who was eating a carrot at this very moment.

I had no shame in my body that I mentally replaced that carrot with my dick in my imagination. Her lips wrapped around it gently before she nibbled her little piece off. My dick was with my head in this moment. Both of us wanted those lips on my cock.

When her lips lifted into a smirk, I knew I had been caught. Lifting my eyes up to hers, I saw that little crazy glint in them. She licked the carrot seductively, and I swear I even heard a little moan. My lips parted, and my dick was standing up, like a damn dog ready for his treat.

Then she bit the shit out of the carrot.

"Fuck!" I groaned, swearing I could feel that bite on my dick. Without thinking, I covered my crotch in protection. Evil woman.

She laughed, tossing the remains of the poor carrot away and headed toward my chair so she could touch up my face before we started back up. She played dirty; good thing I found that undeniably sexy about her. I just prayed that she only liked to use a tiny bit of teeth while she played with my dick.

After I finished my plate, I washed my hands and went over to drop into my chair for her touch-ups.

Neither one of us said anything, mostly because I was still imagining her biting my cock.

"You doing all right there, Cowboy Casanova?" she asked as she went to work.

"I'm not a cowboy," I grumped, but it seemed she was sticking with this nickname since it was the song she sang back at the bar.

"But you are a casanova. Bet you've slept with a bunch of women here, haven't you?" She was wrong about that, but I didn't feel like correcting her. She had this notion in her head that I was a huge manwhore. I did have sex, lots of it. But I wasn't a manwhore like she was thinking. And even though I wanted her more than anything, I never mixed business and pleasure. I had a reputation for professionalism. You could ask anyone in Hollywood—they would tell you that I never slept with my coworkers, something most actors and actresses couldn't say.

Don't shit where you work. It was the easiest way to fuck up a movie. The lover gets angry and makes your life miserable. No, thank you. But everything was different with her. I wanted to screw her into an orgasm coma for sure, but I also wanted to make her banana pancakes in the morning, wash her hair in my shower, and rub her feet after the long days of her standing on set. I actually liked being in relationships. I wasn't a serial dater, but when I found someone I could spend time with other than just sex, I would.

Alessandra just wasn't getting it.

"All right. Go get dirty." She shooed me towards the muddy set ahead of me. I was about to go crawling through the mud, on the run from a creature that was trying to eat me after having escaped his prison.

The scene was easy enough, and when the day was done, I went back to my trailer and took a long shower.

Continuing my little routine since I first saw Alessandra, my hand wrapped around my cock and I began to stroke myself. Instead of imagining her lips around my cock—because carrot— I thought of her hands pressed up against the glass of the shower while I grabbed her perfectly tanned tits in my head, fucking her so hard that her screams could be heard outside the trailer.

She'd ruined my daydreams of her mouth on my cock forever. Only the real-life sight would erase the damage she did.

Her pussy would be tight, and would suck me in with every thrust. Her screams would be music to my ears; when I pulled out and flipped her around, her eyes would be wild with want. My hands would lift her up by that round, apple-shaped ass of hers, and I'd be back in her before she even tried to beg me for it.

Those nails of hers would be digging into my back, and her hot breath would be on my lips. Knowing her, she would probably bite my lip, or something that would cause a slight tinge of pain, but would also be my undoing.

Cum shot out from my cock, then began spiraling down the drain.

"Fucking hell." My orgasm was strong, and I felt my knees start to buckle. My other hand shot out to hold myself up on the glass.

After the final spasms subsided, I just stood under the spray and thought about what I was doing wrong.

My fingers started to prune so I jumped out of the shower and dried off, throwing on a pair of swim trunks. I wanted to hit the pool when I made it back to the little bungalow I had rented for the duration of the movie. The whole drive through the Hollywood night to my residence was filled with thoughts of what else I could do to win Alessandra over.

She wasn't like most of the women around me. She was smart, and spirited. But she seemed closed off, for some reason, toward me. Aside from the whole thought that I'm a manwhore in her eyes, I couldn't think of what else it could be. I was charming, good-looking, witty. But maybe she wanted the deeper side. Not the Hollywood heartthrob; the Joel that liked to surf and hang by the fire pit with Killian and his love, Livia. I wasn't a big attention-seeker when I didn't have to be. But with the job comes attention, whether you want it or not. Maybe that was something she didn't like.

Shit, I wish I knew what it was.

As I parked my red-and-black Bugatti Veyron that Killian had delivered to me a few months ago, I tried to think of what Alessandra saw when she was around me.

The Hollywood Joel, or just Joel? Maybe it was time I showed her what being with the real me would be like.

I walked in the house, threw my wallet, keys, and phone on the table, then headed straight for the water.

Chapter Three

Alessandra

"Seriously, kid?"

All I could do was sit there on the couch with my head in my hands. It's happening. And I didn't like it.

"You should have knocked!" Jenson, my thirteen-year-old son, yelled at me.

"Well, maybe you should have turned on a light, so I'd know you were in there. Or geez, hung a tie on the door or something!" My voice rose as well. I tried so hard to get the image of my son jerking off out of my head. I was mortified. I knew it was going to happen at some point. I mean, he's thirteen now, he's going to be into girls, and his penis. We'd already had the talk years ago, but he wasn't into it so much. But obviously things have changed. My little boy, with his silky black hair and dark blue eyes, that used to play with his action figures in the tub, is now choking the chicken in our shared bathroom.

"Shit, I didn't know I was supposed to alert everyone when I wanted to do it." Smart ass. I always wondered where he got that from. Not me, of course.

"Watch your mouth." I lifted my head up and zoomed in on him with the mom look.

"Sorry," he mumbled.

He just stood there awkwardly, and I knew better than to make something like this taboo. The body wasn't something he should be afraid of. I just don't wanna know about it or see it. Simple.

"All right. Look, it's okay, what you did. It's natural. It's just not something I want to see, you know? Do it in your room. Lock the door, or do something that gives me notice that you are not to be disturbed. Deal?" He nodded and walked away, probably feeling pretty embarrassed. I didn't blame him. I wanted to take a big gulp of tequila and forget that whole scene.

I looked at my little wall above the TV that was full of pictures. Me and the kid, as he grew up. I had gotten pregnant with him when I was seventeen. It was a surprise. His dad was excited at first, but then once Jenson was born, the reality of responsibilities set in. He wanted to be an actor, and party, not have to take care of a kid all the time. Selfish. So when he made the move to Hollywood, I pulled up my sweatpants, and became both a mother and father to my son. We had a great life so far.

Our apartment wasn't big. But it was home, and we liked it. Close to the beach, which Jenson and I loved. He had nice friends, and was at a good school. Things were good.

I prayed for years that when he hit that teenage stage we wouldn't have problems and so far it was okay. He wasn't giving me any more attitude than he normally did. He still dressed nice. Not hipster, or like a punk. Just jeans, a shirt, or sometimes gym shorts.

I wasn't ready for this. I don't think many parents are. I guess I should just be thankful I don't have a girl right now. I was a pure handful, so that would be karma hitting me.

A yawn took over my face, and I realized how tired I was. Work was killer, being on my feet all day, then coming home to make dinner, and clean up the house some. I wanted nothing more than to take a hot bath, with a bottle of something. I heard Jenson's favorite movie coming from his room and knew he was settling in for the night, too.

Deciding to take that bath, and chill, I went into my room and changed my day's clothes out for my robe. Before heading into the bathroom, I opened the cabinet beneath the kitchen sink and grabbed the bleach.

I couldn't sit anywhere in there right now without at least wiping it down. God knows how long this has been going on, and what it would look like in there if I had a black light. I didn't wanna know.

Once the tub was as clean as I could get it, I started the water and waited for the little shower tub to fill up. It didn't take long; by the time I placed the cleaner under the sink and grabbed the bottle of tequila, it was about done.

I tried to fit as much of my five-foot-eight frame into the water as I could. It was either leave my top half out of the water and have my knees covered, or bend my knees and slouch to cover my chest with water.

At least I could take a bath in clean water. I had a cousin back in Rio de Janeiro that didn't have that luxury. So I smiled, and took a sip from the bottle.

"You, take those men to the warehouse; I'll find another way." An all-too-familiar voice echoed under the door, bringing my thoughts back to work despite my best efforts.

Jenson's favorite character was one that Joel had played. He watched the movie all the time. Tried to be like that character—heroic, athletic. He even asked if I could start prepping him meals so he could bulk up like Joel did in the movie. That lasted all of a week, when I told him he had to eat lots of healthy proteins and lift weights. One slice of pizza on our movie night, and he was a goner. It was hard to avoid the thoughts of Joel, with his voice playing in my house.

He was something else, and I kinda was starting to like our little game with each other. Still, I wouldn't have sex with him. He was all Hollywood. With his good looks and charm he thought could get him anything. For the most part, it worked. I just wasn't falling for it.

The tequila was making its way home in my veins, fooling me into believing the water was warmer than it was. I felt calm and cozy. Bed was calling my name now. Tomorrow was going to be another long day of fighting off Joel's idiotic attempts to seduce me.

Chapter Four

Alessandra

Morning came all too quickly.

After getting the kid off to school, and grabbing a yogurt parfait in the parking lot, I walked with my head held high to the trailer to get everything set up for today.

Kandi, the girl with the blue hair who did the costumes, was finishing up her choices when I opened the door.

"Morning," I said politely. She wasn't a super nice person, as far as I could tell. She just popped her bubble in my direction and went back to putting outfits together.

"Okay, then," I mumbled under my breath and went to my station. Today's scenes were pretty easy. Well, for me. Joel was going to have to do some stunt fighting, which I found out he trained to do so he could perform them all himself. No stunt double in this movie. I was slightly impressed by the amount of work he put into these films. No one could say Joel Kline wasn't a hard worker.

"All right, ladies, let's make this mug into a hero." Joel opened the door and held his arms out, like we were his fairy godmothers that were just going to wave a wand and fix him up to save the world.

I rolled my eyes, and Kandi just popped another bubble in her mouth. That had to exhaust her jaw muscles, chewing gum all day like that. I swear I never saw her without a piece smacking in there.

Joel made a face that expressed he wanted to laugh at her lack of response toward him as he walked over to his chair in front of me.

"Looking tired there, Lips. Long night?" He closed his eyes, ready for our routine. I cleaned his face, and started putting the right makeup on him. He needed to look a little bruised today, so I added nice blues, purples, and greens on his cheek.

"Just a little bit," I answered honestly while focusing on my job.

"I'm sure you got chicks you can talk to, but I can be a pretty good sounding board, if you ever need to vent it out."

I pulled back to look at him, to see if there was any hint of mischief in his face, but there was none. That was a genuine sentiment, and I was a little surprised by it, as simple as his words were.

"Thanks."

Somehow, we spent our time at my station in peace. He didn't make a pass at me, and even though my battle gear was on for it, I didn't need to deflect him at all.

He left to change into his gear, and walked to set without a single flirt at me.

By the time our lunch break came, I was weirded out.

"Okay, what's the deal? You're not being your pervy self to me. Are you on drugs?" I looked into his eyes for some hint of why he was acting weird.

He let out a short laugh while making himself a plate of food.

"Miss me trying to bed you?" He smirked, and I felt better. He was still himself, just calmer today for some reason, thank goodness.

"Of course, not, I just figured if you kept all that cheesy energy inside, you might burst. And there would go my job. Can't have that."

He took a big bite of his sandwich, and walked back to his chair, leaving me standing there, still curious as to what he was up to.

I made myself a plate and went over to sit next to him. We ate silently, and then it was time to get back to work.

"How old are you?" he asked, breaking the quiet with a question. A normal question while I touched up his "bruised" cheek.

"Thirty."

"Me, too," he replied. I already knew that about him, though.

"Favorite food?" He asked another question.

"What's with the twenty-one questions?"

"Just asking harmless questions, Lips. Maybe if we got to know each other a little better, we wouldn't be pulling each other's hair on the playground. Maybe we could play nice with each other."

His reasoning made sense. Us bantering back and forth was starting to gain the attention of those around us. We could be civil. It's what I wanted in the first place.

"Fine," I sighed.

"Coxinhas. My mom's recipe though." My mouth watered, thinking about biting into one of those little fried balls of goodness.

"Never had them. I'll have to check them out. I'm a pizza man, myself. Back in the day I used to toss pizzas during high school."

I finished the final touches on his face and told him to open his eyes.

"So you're a pizza tosser. Cute." I giggled, trying to imagine him covered in flour, throwing big, stretched-out pieces of dough in the air.
"Oh, yeah, I'm a great tosser." He smiled, and I laughed harder, shooing him off to do his job. I wanted to make some other jokes at him, but stopped myself. Joking was harmless, but letting myself feel comfortable around Joel was not. It would be too easy to let myself go with him if he kept this nicer side up.

Maybe I needed to find a man. Take the edge off.

I sat in my chair again and watched Joel fight off some warriors on set. He was being thrown around like he was nothing. The wires attached to his waist helped. But this was going to be an epic fight scene in the completed movie, for sure.

"Couple of us from set were thinking about going out to The Bean tonight. You wanna join us?" Kandi had snuck up beside me and at the sound of her words, I about jumped out of my skin.

"Jesus Christ!" My hand was over my heart, trying to steady the fast beat.

"Chill out,c hicarita." She popped a bubble and watched the scene in front of us.

"Sorry, you just haven't spoken to me previously, so it kinda felt like you shouted at me. About made me pee."

"Yeah, I've been on the rag. You know how it is, makes you a little extra bitchy." She shrugged. I guess I could see that. Ever since Jenson was born, my periods were a little more crampy than usual. And of course my hormones kinda went all over the place, too. So I get it.

"What time?" I could use a little fun. Jenson has been wanting to stay at his friend's house. I could shoot him a text. He'd be thrilled, especially after last night.

"Eight. They have a pretty good set playing tonight."

"I think I can swing it. Thanks." I smiled at her, and she just nodded before walking off to one of the other people on set.

A night for adult fun was just what I needed. I watched as Joel's shirt ripped open, showing off all his rippling muscles.

Definitely think I need to get laid tonight.

Chapter Five

Joel

My face was itchy as hell.

My fingers ran through the fake beard I'd put on so I could remain anonymous while out with the film crew. Nothing ruins a good time like being surrounded by a mob and cameras. I tended to do this whenever we were out during filming, which is why people still invited me out to chill with them.

"Anybody else coming?" I asked Mark, one of the sound boom guys.

"Uh, I think Alessandra and Tina are coming. Right, Kandi?" He looked towards Blue Pop. Kandi was her real name, but I liked my nickname in my head for her better.

"Yep." She set her gum on the side of her beer, and took a sip, not once taking her eyes off the band playing ahead of us.

The Bean was a little coffee bar, but at night they had local bands perform. People could come hang out, nurse something stronger than coffee, and listen to the tunes. Very laid back setting.

"Hey, guys. Sorry, traffic was a mess."

I looked up to see Alessandra setting her purse down and pulling out the chair next to me.

"Hi." She smiled at me, not recognizing who I was. Interesting. It had been a whole twenty-four hours since I had riled her little feathers a bit. I wondered how long it would take for her to realize who I was.

"Hi. Randy." I changed my voice to sound more like a cowboy.

"Alessandra." She smiled and held out her hand to shake. I took her hand in mine and loved the way it fit perfectly. Even though I wanted to keep holding on, my fingers let go of hers.

All seven pairs of eyes at the table around us were watching my little charade with Alessandra. Some of them were curious; the others were about ready to burst out with laughter.

"I haven't seen you around set; what do you do?" She was all smiles and niceness. It was strange for me to see her this way. Having a normal conversation. If she knew it was me, her walls would be up faster than a kid with his first titty magazine.

"I'm a tech guy." Her head tilted slightly, like she was trying to place my face but couldn't. I must have done a really good job with my fake beard, and chose a good hat.

"Cool beans." She let whatever thought she had go and ordered a Corona when the waitress came over to get her order. Another girl who I'm pretty sure was Leighton's assistant stole her attention, and I sat there thinking about how I could use this to my advantage.

Suddenly Alessandra's phone started ringing My Hero by Foo Fighters, a song I knew very well. Considering it was the song that played when I saved the day in my last film. I was a super hero, and boy did I eat that shit up. Was she a fan of my work? More questions just kept piling up the more I was around her.

"Excuse me," she told the table and took the call outside. I wanted more time around her, and even though stupid, to see whose ringtone that was.

"Hey, Mark, give me one of your cigarettes and lighter for a minute." I kinda demanded them but he just shrugged and handed them to me. Everyone was over my charade, for now at least, they were just enjoying the show.

I stood up quickly and walked out to where I saw the apple of my eye talking on the phone.

Quietly, my arm pressed the door open so I wouldn't disturb her. Playing the part, I put the cigarette in my mouth and lit it. I'd had to smoke for roles before, so the action was easy. Never got in the habit of it, though. It was purely a prop for me.

"Jenson. I will talk to you later about it, okay?"

Jenson?

Was he a lover? She never wore a ring, so it certainly wasn't a husband.

"I love you, too. Bye." She pressed the end button, and I turned my head towards the sky like I wasn't just listening into her conversation.

"Oh, Christ on a cracker!" she exclaimed, jumping seeing me so close. It was sort of amusing, seeing her like that. Cute, really. I would have thought she would have ninja-chopped someone who scared her.

"Sorry, ma'am." I took a drag and blew it out towards the stars.

"It's all right. I was just distracted." That smile grew on her lips, and she started to walk back towards the door. I started to panic, not wanting her to leave yet.

"It's gonna work out, you know. You're a pretty girl. Whoever he is, it'll be good." The words flew out, and I wasn't sure what they meant.

"Uh, who?" She looked confused.

"They guy on the phone. Your man." Maybe I was digging for information, something to give me a hint that she was seeing someone.

"Oh." She looked at me, still with a confused look on her face. But then she took a step towards me.

"I don't know. I just feel so stupid." Now what the hell was she talking about?

"I keep taking him back, even though he cheats on me. I just love him so much, but it still hurts." She looked down, like my little tigress was about to cry. Hell no to that shit.

"He's a fucking dickwad who deserves his ass beaten." Accent was gone, but she didn't register it, obviously very upset. God, I can't believe this. She was with someone who had her love, and he was cheating on her! I was so pissed right now. I would get his name from her tomorrow in the trailer, and then I would hunt his ass down. I knew ways to torture people, thanks to the horror movie I did a few years ago.

"That's very sweet. I just wish I could get him back. You know, make him hurt like he hurts me. Maybe he wouldn't do it anymore. I should just cheat on him."

The end of the cigarette had burned and fell onto my boot, and I swear I heard it hit the leather. My mouth parted slightly, thinking about what she might be insinuating.

"I know this is way out there," she started to say, but then stopped.

"No, I'm sorry. It's too inappropriate." She started to turn, but I wasn't having that shit. Not now, no fucking way. I grabbed her arm and spun her back around, pulling her body close to mine. Away from the glass of the bar, no one could see that there was zero space between us.

"Say it," I whispered against her hair, feeling her body shiver in my arms. I felt a slight sting of her nails biting into my forearms. My fantasy was coming to fruition.

"I just thought that maybe…" She looked up into my eyes, and I wished that she was really looking at me as Joel and not this hillbilly tech guy.

"You want to make him hurt. You want him to think of you getting punished by my dick over and over. Screaming out my name. Say it," I growled, feeling like I wanted to take her right there. She was pulling out the alpha male in me. I wanted to claim her against the wall so that shithead man of hers would know who she really belonged to.

Her head leaned in closer, and then stopped just before my lips. I would let her take that final step.

"I want you to..." She closed her eyes, and was almost there. Fuck, this was happening!

"To..." she whispered and I felt her lips caress mine gently. Not really a kiss, but she was a centimeter away from it.

"To show me how you got this ridiculous thing to stay on your face. I mean seriously, I think I will need to do all your disguises from now on if this is how you do it."

Uh, what?

Her body pulled away from mine in a fit of laughter. What the fuck just happened?

Alessandra was laughing hysterically in front of me. Like, full-on, stitch-in-her-stomach laughter. Unbelievable.

"You knew it was me?" I felt played. Which was pretty hypocritical, since I was sort of playing her, too, but whatever. These are my feelings.

"Really, Joel? I look at your face every day, up close and personal. You really think I wouldn't recognize you?" Her laughter was calming down, but those feelings in my stomach hadn't gone away. I schooled my face.

"You could have been a pretty good actress. Although I knew that you'd figured it out. I just wanted to see if I could get you to kiss me. Since pretty boys aren't your type, thought I'd try the cowboy." Even though that was a complete lie, she bought it.

"No thanks, Cowboy Casanova." She smiled and walked back into the bar.

Fuck, now I was never going to live down that name. But at least she didn't see the real emotions that were stirring in my gut from our play.

I walked back in with all the swagger I could muster up, feeling nothing like the man that smiled and joked with his coworkers. For the first time, I felt like I was in uncharted waters with Alessandra. I wasn't giving up, but for the night I would let myself feel vulnerable to what this girl was doing to me. She had me up in knots, consuming all my thoughts, and feeding that desire to make her mine.

Chapter Six

Alessandra

"All done." I pulled back my cotton pad from Joel's face and he immediately jumped up and went back to work on set without one word uttered to me.

Whatever. I wasn't too thrilled with him right now, either. He was screwing with me last night, so I screwed him back. His butt-hurt feelings didn't make me feel any better, but seriously. He was all too eager to play along and get me into his bed.

In a way, I know it was all a joke. And I'm not sure why I played along. But the whole day today, he had been putting on a front with me. He would smile, and look every bit Joel Kline on the outside, but I saw it in his eyes. He knew he shouldn't have played with me. And he didn't like it that I played back. The player got played, so to speak, and he didn't like that it was his own fire that burned him.

I watched him as he rested in a space ship whose course was set for Earth. Of course, it wouldn't make it there, that would be too easy. But right now, he was talking to the reader who was slowly falling in love with him. You could hear the sadness in his voice. The loneliness.

He was a good actor. I felt like he meant every word he said, even though it was scripted.

When Leighton yelled cut, Joel just sat in the fake ship for a few minutes while everyone around went about their business. When his eyes finally travelled my way, I waved him over, and he nodded.

As he jumped out of the ship and walked over to me, everything in my head started to weigh on me.

"Hey, can we talk?" Even though I didn't really do anything more wrong than he did, I was still his lead artist, and he could make my life miserable if he wanted to. Not that I thought he would, but the air between us needed to be cleared.

"Sure." He looked at me, and waited.

"I think last night got carried away from both of us. I'm sorry for my end." There.

"I'm sorry, too. Who's Jenson?" His voice held slight malice at the mention of Jenson's name. Oh boy. Did he really think I was with a guy that cheated on me?

"My thirteen-year-old son. He was at a friend's house last night and wanted to know if we could go surfing this weekend." I was nervous mentioning my son to him.

When he took in my words, his expression was almost comical.

"Your son?"

"Yeah, my son, Jenson."

"I didn't know you had a son; why haven't you mentioned him?" He sounded hurt, but that was just too weird, so I ignored it.

"Didn't know we were friends like that. Last time I checked, you just wanted to get into my pants." He rolled his eyes, and it was sort of a cute reaction. But it was Joel. He was cute no matter what he did.

"Well, we are friends now. You wanna talk about shit, you can call me anytime." Without asking, he reached into my pocket and grabbed my phone. I didn't have any lock on it, so one swipe and he was typing away. I didn't protest. I should have, but I didn't. When he was obviously up to something other than just putting in his number, which should have only taken a few seconds, I tried to get it back from his greedy hands.

"Okay, what are you doing now?" I lunged for the phone, and he held it above his head, still up to something.

"Seriously, what are we, twelve? This is stuff my son would do." He stuck his tongue out at me.

"Real nice."

"There you go. Now you can call your new bestie anytime." He smiled and sauntered off, looking pleased with himself.

"You're not my bestie!" I hissed at him and followed behind. He grabbed an orange from the food table and started peeling.

"Can't let me go, huh, Lips?" I huffed and walked away. Jesus, I swear he lived to screw with me in any way he could.

The rest of the day went by quickly, and we actually were done pretty early. As soon as I got home, I gathered our surf gear together so when Jenson got home from school we could grab some waves before the sun set.

It was all worth it to see the smile on his face when he saw I was ready with our boards, my wet suit on, and beach bag in my hand. He put his fist in the air in triumph and zipped off to his room to throw his suit on. Together we headed toward the beach.

We were all tied up and ditched our bag in the sand, heading straight for the water. Surfing and his love of the water was something he got from me. No matter what we had been through, the water always took away the stress of life. We had gotten in a good half hour of shredding the waves before I heard Jenson yell out to me.

"Got a man in a gray suit!" He started paddling towards the beach calmly, and every other surfer who heard him, did the same. Wanting to be with my baby and not risk fate more than I was, I paddled in as well. No reason to be out looking like a tasty turtle when there was a shark sighting.

"You really saw one, kid?" a tanned surfer asked Jenson.

"Yeah, looked like a fourteen-footer." Jenson loved sharks. He wanted so badly for his birthday to go to the big aquarium in Monterey Bay and swim with the creatures. I still wasn't sold on the idea.

"Nice. Good call then, kid. And good job with the lingo. Didn't freak the tourists out." The surfer ruffled Jenson's hair, and walked off. He tried to fix his messed-up black do, but failed. The salty sea water was acting like gel, keeping it in disarray.

"You wanna just hang out?" I asked, trying to gauge what he wanted to do. I was kinda getting hungry, but if he wanted to hang out on the beach, I would be down for whatever he wanted.

He looked around and shrugged.

"Food sounds good."

"Sharky's?" It was a nice little beach restaurant. It had a rack for our boards, and we could sit under little umbrellas to stay out of the sun.

He mumbled a yes, but I understood it. Teenager speak was happening to him. One word answer here, another grunt there. Thankfully I was tuning in to it, and could interpret.

Sharky's was pretty busy, but we managed to snag a table, and the waitress took our order. We always got the same thing—he got a burger with ketchup, mustard,and pickles, with a side of fries. I ordered fish and chips. Something about being on the water always made me want a basket of fried goodness. Not sure why, it was just what I always craved.

Our food came out pretty quickly, and Jenson dove in like an animal. I swore I raised him to not make such a mess, but he seemed to always prove me wrong.

"Just when I didn't think my day could get any better." My whole body froze, hearing that voice. Oh dear God, please don't let it be him.

Chapter Seven

Joel

The look on Alessandra's face was pure horror, an expression I found completely adorable. I just wanted to smush her cheeks with my hands and kiss her lips so hard.

She looked at me and blinked, most likely hoping I would disappear. Hell to the no on that one, baby. Then her head whipped towards the teenage boy she was eating with.

It had to be her son, and he was staring at me like I was his biggest hero. Honestly, both of their faces were priceless.

"Care if I join you guys?" I started to pull out a chair when both of them started talking. Alessandra was saying "Yes," and her son saying, "Fuck no!" Alessandra's head whipped back to her son and she swatted him on the arm in a very motherly way.

"Mouth!" she barked, giving him an eye.

"Seriously? I'm allowed right now to curse. Do you know who this is?" He gave her attitude right back. Yep, he was most definitely her son.

"Thanks. You guys get some water time in this afternoon?" I plopped down in my seat and waited for our lucky server to come back our way.

"Yeah, we did. It was sick! But then I saw the man in the gray suit, and we hightailed it out of there. It was like a fourteen-footer, dude." The kid rambled on while his mom just looked uncomfortable as hell.

"Nice. I once saw a twenty-footer by my house in La Jolla." I grabbed Alessandra's cup and took a sip, just for the reaction I would get from her. She didn't disappoint—her face said there was going to be hell to pay for all of this.

"No way!!" he said excitedly, then he schooled his face.

"I mean, that's pretty cool." Heh. Trying to be all nonchalant about it, a true teenager. These two. I could be around them all day and never be bored.

Another kid yelled out to Jenson, and Alessandra excused him to go say hello. The waitress came right before Alessandra had her chance to question me or give me some sort of attitude. Saved! She stared at me as I pretended not to know what I wanted, and wasted time asking the waitress about what she liked on the menu. If steam could come out of my girl's ears, it would be.

I ended up ordering a burger and fries, sending the starry-eyed waitress on her way to put in the order.

"What the hell are you doing here? Are you stalking me now?" The words just flew out of her mouth, and with a tinge of that accent I found so attractive. She glanced at her son, who was pointing subtly at me, then her eyes came back to my face.

"Yeah, it's my new hobby. I follow you around the traffic of Los Angeles, hanging in the trees, waiting to catch a peek at your tits while you change. I pretty much live outside your window." I smile the whole time I'm spinning my story, which she knew was all crap, too.

"I honestly was just walking towards the surf when I saw you and had to come over. The water is my second home, and today was such a nice day. As you know, we don't always get out before the sun sets." It was as simple as that. No conspiracy here.

Those walls of hers were up high, but I could see she was willing to put down a window.

"Oh. We like the water, too." I liked that, very much in fact.

"You surf too?" If she said yes, I might have to ask her to marry me right now.

"Yeah, it's something Jenson and I like to do together." My hand reached out for hers, and my mouth just opened.

"That's it, Alessandra, you are the woman for me. Marry me?" If I was being honest with myself, I would have to admit that if she said yes, I would probably go through with it. I wasn't in love. But this was a woman I felt like I could be around for years upon years, and never get bored. She was so refreshing, and everything about her I have discovered I really liked. A girl who surfs? Dream come true.

"Yeah,sure. You wouldn't last five minutes with me as your wife." She scoffed, and I felt my dick start to stir, thinking about the fun we would have living in the same house together. Then her son came back with his friend.

"Hey. Um, can I get a picture?" asked Jenson's friend, who was a little pudgier than Jenson but had this goofy grin on his face and twinkles in his brown eyes.

"Sure thing." I took a fun picture with the kid and soon my food arrived at the table.

Jenson rejoined us, and we talked about surfing, and how he's been dying to swim with the sharks up in Monterey Aquarium. He really enjoyed all things ocean. Every once in a while, during our little dinner, Alessandra would pipe up and tell a story of Jenson's childhood years. I think it was just a mom thing, and of course Jenson would turn pink and try to shush her. He never once asked how I knew his mom, and she didn't discuss it, either.

When it was time to leave, we said our goodbyes in a civil manner. Which was not what I preferred. I would have rather pulled her into my arms, dipped her down, and kissed her hard, so she would think of our kiss during our separation. Instead there was a "thanks for hanging out with us" from the kid, a "bye" from her, and I said a "see you tomorrow."

They both hitched their boards under their arms, and headed towards the road. I wondered if they lived around here. It wasn't the best of areas, but it wasn't super shitty either.

"Are you going to date Joel?" I heard Jenson ask his mom while they walked off. She didn't answer, and he gave her his opinion, which was pretty awesome.

"You so should. Then we can go surfing together!" I had won the kid over, easy-peasy. Now his mom just needed to come on board, which seemed to be the hardest part. But slowly, I could break down her walls. It would work. It had to work.

The sun was just about to hit the ocean, so there wasn't much point of me diving in. Instead I took my sandals off and walked along the shore, aware that there were people taking pictures of me the whole way. I didn't pay them any mind, but then it clicked in my head.

Maybe that was something Alessandra had an issue with—the fame. She wouldn't want to be in every magazine as my play toy, let alone her son getting caught up in the mix. Stuff like that could cause problems, that I knew from experience.

But how was I going to keep that from happening? I was who I was. I enjoyed my life; I loved my job. It was my passion to act, bringing happiness to people for the cost of a movie ticket and maybe some popcorn.

Figuring it was time to head back to my little cottage, I thought about an addition to my new game plan of winning Alessandra.

Maybe her whole offer to help with my disguises could come into play. She can't complain about being in the limelight with me if no one knows it's me. Could be fun.

So many thoughts were running through my head. I would make this work.

After a dip in the pool, and I was all cleaned up, I relaxed on the couch and popped in a movie. I loved movies. I didn't just enjoy making them, I truly loved watching them. I love watching the acting, and knowing what they went through to create that part. I love watching the story happen. Movies were something that made my mind go blank, and allowed me to be in the moment to enjoy them. Not many things had that effect on me. Before I knew it, I woke up with my alarm. It was time to make some magic happen. And by magic, I mean make Alessandra like me.

Chapter Eight

Alessandra

I was dying.

This was the end for me. Jenson would figure out how to survive on his own. He was a bright boy. He would find a wife someday, and I was going to miss it, but he would know I loved him with all my heart. I tried my best.

"Shit, Alessandra. Are you all right?" Joel was suddenly in front of me, his face full of concern. Maybe I should have given him a chance. At least for one night. A secret night of passion.

"I'm dying." My voice was hoarse. I knew the end was near. So much pain.

"Seriously, Alessandra. Tell me what the fuck is going on. You look like shit, but you aren't dying. And people say I'm an actor." He was teasing me. It wasn't nice to do when someone was about to go into the light. My eyes closed, and my hands clenched around my stomach. My fingers were gripping my shirt so hard that the material was close to tearing.

"My uterus is revolting against me for not having another baby," I groaned, wanting nothing more than to go lie on the bed in peace and wait for death to take me.

"I see. Should have taken me up on my sex offer; I could have cured that problem for you." He was fucking with me again, and really, hasn't he been around any woman while she was on her period? We were bitches not to be fucked with. True to the almighty PMS, I went from debilitated, dying woman, to Xena the Warrior Princess.

"Really! I don't want your baby! My uterus has been without a child for thirteen years; she's gonna live. Only like, what, fifteen to twenty-five more years, and she will shrivel up. I don't need your dick knocking me up! I am a strong, independent woman! I can handle it!"

Somehow in my rant I had stood and was now looking at him in the eye. He was holding in his laughter. I scoffed and pushed him into his chair so I could get this over with.

"You're lucky I don't feel like losing my job,otherwise I would make you look like Ursula from *The Little Mermaid*." I put my hair back into a ponytail and met his eyes in the mirror.

"What?" He was just staring at me. Not with fear, like I wanted, but with something suspiciously like adoration. Ugh.

"You're adorable. Need anything? Some Advil? Chocolate? Tampons? I heard milk helps with symptoms of PMS."

"Yeah, I need to put makeup on your face so you can get out of mine. You're irritating me." He sort of wasn't, but I was too far gone with the sickness to come back now.

He continued to smile, but he stayed quiet so I could do my job. Once he was finished, Kandi got him dressed, and we all walked over towards the set.

"Man, it's hot out here." I started fanning myself, feeling flushed and overheated. I looked up at the sky, which was overcast. Obviously I was going through a hot flash or something. Everyone just looked at me like I was nuts, but kept on walking. I knew that the first day of my period was the worst. The pain, the crazy, and I prayed hard that my other symptom didn't emerge. Subtly, I looked to the side at Joel walking.

He looked delectable, just like always.

"Still not gonna do it." I turned my head back to the stage door and repeated that mantra over and over.

Joel quickly went to work, and Kandi and I just stood there watching.

"You look like a hobo," Kandi commented, calling me out on my non-effort.

"Yeah, well, I got my period." I shrugged. I was rocking my cut-off boyfriend capris and loose shirt, with flip-flops.

"Gotcha. I got a stash of chocolate back at the trailer, along with other goods, if you need it. Blue bag behind all the clothes." She popped a bubble then walked off. Sweet girl.

We worked hard for the next few hours, and when they gave us an hour break so they could change up the set a little, I ran back to the trailer, took care of business in the bathroom, and sought out that blue bag Kandi said she had.

"Heck yeah." There it was. I didn't wanna rob her completely, so I grabbed two Snickers bars and some Advil.

Once I was settled on the couch, and the liquid pill was starting to take effect, I dove into those chocolate bars, not even pretending to save one for later. Soon a smile started to appear on my face, and I felt happier. Chocolate really was a cure for all that ails. I was basking happily in my thoughts of chocolate when the door opened.

Then it hit me. No, no!

"Hey, just wanted to check on you. I brought donuts in case you were hungry for sugar." Joel was being sweet, and it was the final nail in the coffin.

My other symptom of PMS was happening.

I was horny. It happened every damn time. But I usually managed with my little bullet at the house. One orgasm, and I was good for the rest of the week. It was just this first damn day! I was like Dr. Jekyll and Mr. Hyde.

"I'm feeling better," I mumbled as I checked the corners of my mouth for chocolate. He looked relieved, then sat down next to me. Putting the donuts on the small table next to the couch.His chest was so broad, and I could see through the thin shirt he was wearing. Being attracted to him had never been my issue, and right now I was feeling that desire rise up like a tsunami.

"Good. Haven't killed anyone though, right? I'll be your alibi if you need it." He was messing with me, as was his thing to do. But I was not in the playing mood. My breasts were feeling heavy and in need of some kneading. My brain was short circuiting, and only one thing was on my mind—touching him.

"I haven't," I answered and brought my hand up to his hair. The softness of it felt like heaven in my fingers. He did have good hair. I always thought his little gray patch in the front was hot.

"Uh, you sure you're okay there?" He was looking right at me, and I inched closer.

"I do have a problem. And as much as I don't wanna go there, I really can't stop myself." I leaned in and closed my eyes.

He pulled away.

"Are you coming on to me?" He looked at me like I was crazy. I was. All those little thoughts I'd have about him and his looks, or the thoughts I'd have about him in bed, were all running through my mind right now like my own personal porn gif. My walls had given my body a temporary pass, thanks to my hormones running wild. "Maybe." My nails ran over his scalp, and his eyes closed briefly, enjoying the feeling. Good. I was a wildcat in all matters sex. Not that I would be having sex with him. That wouldn't be good, plus it would just make a mess everywhere. No, I just needed to grind on him, touch him, have him touch me. That would be enough, and I would be good.

He still hadn't said anything, and I knew he wanted me, so I leaned in and pressed my lips to his, giving into the attraction. Maybe deep down I knew I could fight off my hormones, but I was giving up. I would think about it later. I had Joel Kline at my fingertips, and I needed him right now.

Chapter Nine

Joel

Holy. Fucking. Shit.

Alessandra's lips were on mine.

And I didn't want her right now, not like this. I know how women are when they're on the rag. I have two sisters that tried to kill me one minute then wanted me to hold them while they cried when they were on theirs. That was also worse because they were always on it at the same time. Pure torture. So Alessandra seemed to be one that suffered heavily with all the symptoms, including being a cat in heat. I wished I could be an asshole that just let her have her way with me as she clearly wished.

But I wanted her not under the influence, if you will. I wanted her to gladly let me in her life. Willingly. Not just because she had a glitch in her system that temporarily shut down her shields.

"Hold on." I pulled back and tried to get some space between us, but she was on me in a second.

Everything I had thought about her was true. She was all fire and passion. God, I couldn't wait to have her, but I'd wait until she came to me for real. Her lips crashed against mine, and her teeth scraped my bottom lip, making it really hard for me to push her away.

"Not like this. I want you so bad. But not like this. We both know you wouldn't be doing this if your hormones weren't wreaking havoc on you right now." She was looking at me in shock. I know, sweetheart, gentleman Joel Kline wasn't one that everyone got to meet.

"God, I'm such an idiot." Shit. Maybe I shouldn't be around women when they were vulnerable. She looked hurt, but not by me. She was upset with herself. Her hands went to her face in shame.

"In due time, Lips. Soon you will be looking at me with a little twinkle in your eyes. Then you will want me to open your lady flower and gently caress your soft petals." I tweaked my words to make her laugh. It worked. She was focusing on how much of a doofus I was, versus how she threw herself at me.

"You will be shouting from the balcony your love of me. Oh, Joel Kline! My Joel Kline!" I kept going. Making her smile was all I cared about right now. I didn't give a shit what people thought of me, and I was a goof sometimes.

"You're ridiculous." She smacked my arm lightly, like she did to her son yesterday. That was something.

"It's going to happen, Alessandra my sweet."

She rolled her eyes but I could tell that she was thankful for the change of subject and making light of things. She probably would have stewed in her feelings, and after the day ends, she still might. But for now, she smiled, and I was happy that I was the one putting that happiness on her face.

"Probably about time to get back to work. You need a few minutes?" I stood and held out a hand for her. She took it and looked around.

"Maybe a few; I'll be on set shortly to touch up your face." She let go of my hand and looked at herself in the mirror, trying to fix her appearance. She looked fine as hell to me; I liked her more casual wear. Her ass looked plump and perfect in those cutoffs. I wish I had permission to smack it or cup it at least. I would be all over that ass. Feeling brave, I smacked her ass anyway, and took off towards the door. It wasn't a nice sexy smack, but more like one that could be used as evidence, with my fingerprints in her luscious tan skin.

"Ah! What the hell! Oh my God, that stings!" she cried out, and I heard something hit the wall by the door that I was already exiting. There was my feisty princess. Right before I closed the door, I yelled back to her.

"Your ass looks good in those pants!" I closed the door quickly, not wanting to get hit in the head with anything.

Today was turning out to be a good day. Though nothing major had happened, Alessandra wouldn't be able to completely shut me out anymore. And she learned I wasn't a complete asshole.

The rest of the day moved quickly. I had a brief scare when I thought I twisted my ankle while jumping from one fake rock to another. But after a few stretches, I was good to go. Doing my own stunts was something I took pride in, not all actors liked the work. It took time to learn how to do the moves safely. I actually took a few months of stunt classes during a break in between movies to up my skills. I think the production companies like that, as well. Less people they had to pay, I guess.

"Thanks for today." Alessandra's voice broke past my thoughts, making me spin around towards her. She was all packed to go, but had taken the extra time to say thank you. Things were improving.

"You're welcome. Anytime you need a period buddy, I'm your guy." Sometimes even I shake my head at the shit that comes out of my mouth.

"Right. Well, bye." She turned and fled. Period buddy. Jesus, what had I been smoking? But at least she said bye. Improvements, indeed.

I went back to the trailer to clean up my appearance a bit, and then my phone started to ring while I was in the shower.

I answered it on speakerphone.

"Hello?" I watched the dirt that was in my hair circle the drain.

"Hi, Joel! Guess what?" It was the voice of my best friend's girl, Livia. When she climbed the fence of my home and told me she was going to try to win Killian back, I was happy for them. He deserved a girl like her. She brought him out of the rain and into the sun.

"What?" I smiled, seeing her overly bright face in my head. Then I laughed a little when I thought of Killian's face right now sitting next to her, because, let's face it, he was probably looking like a grumpy old man.

"We went dune buggying in Vegas! It was so much fun. We will all have to go back sometime. Anyway, Killian and I were wondering how everything was going?"

"She works hard for the money."

I heard a scoff on the other line from Killian, and Livia laughed.

"Lovely theme song. I guess you do work hard for all of your millions. You got to work it like you got it, and you definitely got it." The last part of her sentence was to rile up Killian a little, and based on the growl I heard from him, it worked. They wouldn't be on the phone for much longer.

"You guys still coming out to visit next week?" I turned off the water and dried myself off while I heard some rustling around on their end of the phone. Livia squeaked.

"Yep! We will be there. Okay, gotta go, bye, Joel!" The phone clicked off abruptly.

"Good for them," I said to myself and got dressed.

Next week we had a few days off, and Killian, Livia and I had made plans to chill at my house during that time. Pretty much a nice relaxing weekend of surfing, drinks, and doing as little as possible.

The only thing that would make it better is Alessandra. I had a week to make her comfortable enough to accept my offer to chill at my house, or if that failed, I would have to stoop a little low. But I wasn't above using all my tools in the box to get her. Nope. One way or another, she would be there for the weekend.

Chapter Ten

Alessandra

Is it safe to enter the trailer? -Bestie

He was ridiculous. For one, he really did put his name in my phone as "Bestie." I knew it was him because none of my other friends would do that. Two, he was being dramatic about coming in the trailer. I was over the hard days of my perioditis, so I was back to being normal. Aside from bleeding. I couldn't help the little smile from forming as I fired off an answer.

Depends. Think you can handle the beast?- Alessandra

His reply was instant.

I handle the beast in my pants all the time. I think I can handle the one in yours. -Bestie

He opened the door shortly after I read that, and I couldn't do anything but giggle.

"Really? You are something else." He sat in his chair, and I started prepping his face.

"Yeah, but I'm growing on you." He smiled, and all I could think was, he was right. He was growing on me. Which I guess wasn't so bad. He could have taken advantage of me, the way I threw myself at him like I did. Or even give me shit about it, but he wasn't holding it against me. I didn't really know what was happening, but I realized I could let him in a little.

"Jenson can't stop telling his friends that he met you the other day." Meeting his idol was a big deal. He really had been over the moon since then.

"He was a cool dude. You're doing well with him." I felt my insides warm, hearing him say that. I tried really hard to be a good mom to him. Whenever someone told you that you weren't failing miserably as a parent, it made you feel really good. Especially when you're doing it on your own.

"Thanks."

"So I was thinking, I have some friends coming to my house during our weekend off filming. You two should come down, and chill with us," he asked very casually. Like it was every day he asked his makeup artist and her son to stay at his house.

"Um, I'm not sure about that. Don't wanna cramp your style or anything, having a teenager around." Most adults didn't wanna party with a kid around, and those that did were up to no good. I would pass.

"It's nothing like that. Killian and Livia are like family. He's a truck driver, and she is his girlfriend. We are gonna pretty much surf, eat, and chill the whole weekend."

I heard him, but I was still coming to grips on the thought that Joel was more than just a manwhore, or someone that liked to flaunt his money, and fame. If I was being honest, he wasn't like that at all. I'd known him almost two months, and he had yet to do anything that would make him seem like a pompous ass, aside from our initial encounter.

"I'll think about it." I'm pretty sure I was going to say no, but at least I was trying to be better when it came to him. He wasn't a monster.

"Anything I can do to help make that 'think about it' into a 'yes'?" He looked at me and smiled. That smile was starting to make little butterflies flap in my stomach.

"Yeah, be quiet and let me do my job." I smirked, and he closed his eyes and shut up. Stupid cute actor.

I finished his makeup and then he moved onto wardrobe before jumping on the set. Today was going to be a little different than the others. Today he would not be the main man on set—Lana Hamleia, the Hawaiian princess, was making her debut on the stage for the first time. They would be shooting a scene where Lana would see Luc in her dreams.

Nineveh Presley would be playing the princess, and I hadn't had the pleasure of meeting her yet. She didn't have to show up until today, since they hadn't been filming her scenes. But now I was a little curious what she was like.

I'd never heard of her, until this movie. She was an up-and-coming actress, not a known player like Joel.

About a half hour into filming a beautiful woman, who looked like a biracial goddess, walked onto the set. She was wearing a beat-up night gown, that barely covered her slight frame. Her hair was gorgeous! It was a golden color, much like her tan skin, but was wild. I had total hair envy right now. Mine was mostly straight with a few waves here and there. Nineveh had a mix of tight and loose curls flowing behind her as she walked over to a shitty-looking bed. She lay down against the pillow, and Joel stood off to the side, waiting to rush to her in dreamland.

"Okay, Nineveh, remember, you are sleeping fitfully. Then you dream of Luc. And...*Action!*" Leighton started rolling and the action did begin.

It was mesmerizing to watch her in the scene; she was very talented. This movie was going to be her big break. I just knew it. God, I hoped she wasn't a bitch.

"Luc, you're here? But how?" She raced into Joel's arms, and he held her close. They were intertwined for a few minutes before moving to the bed so he could hold her while she talked to him about her day, and then fell asleep.

All-too-familiar feelings churned in my stomach when he held her and was so soft to her. It was so natural to him. And I kinda sort of—but would never say out loud—may be feeling a tinge of jealousy. Which was dumb, because I really didn't want to have him that way.

God, did I?

Was he already working his way under my skin? I'd acknowledged the attraction, but was there a little more to this now? He was nice, and caring, funny, quick-witted, and wasn't too bad to be around.

I liked Joel Kline.

Heaven help me.

His fame was still an issue for me. That, and it was hard to know that it wasn't all an act. Alex, my ex, played me once with his acting skills. I didn't wanna be screwed over by another. Thoughts of my ex hardened me slightly. I would not go through that again. As much as I was warming up to Joel, and even admitted I liked him, I wouldn't go further. Thankfully, no one else besides Tommy, Jenson's friend, had gotten a picture of Joel on the beach while he ate with us. I looked, but only saw some of him walking on the beach afterwards.

I turned off my laptop after that. There were other pictures of him and women that I didn't care to see. One was only a short time after we met at the bar, holding a petite blonde woman in his arms on the beach.

I was feeling so confused. When the final shot was taken for the day, I packed up my stuff and hauled ass. I didn't feel like facing Joel while I was dealing with all of these feelings.

Jenson was doing homework when I got home, and I quickly jumped into the kitchen and whipped us up some homemade hamburger helper.

"How'd filming go today?" Jenson asked, hanging out at the table while I cooked. He had been interested in my job more, now that he knew who I was working with. Putting makeup on people wasn't that cool, in his eyes. But he enjoyed it when I did body paint at festivals, and more creative makeup on sets.

"Pretty good. How was school?" He told me about how he did really well at basketball today, and then started to stuff his face as soon as I set the bowl of food in front of him. He was always eating, and where he put it, I couldn't say. He wasn't super skinny, but he had a high metabolism like his dad. Me? Everything I ate went to my ass or my thighs. I ran at the little gym in my apartment complex when I could, but with filming taking up most of my time, the only exercise I got most days was running back and forth between the trailer and the set. Standing all day helped a little, but I had learned to be proud of my body over the years. I gained forty pounds with my little guy. He was a big baby. So I have stretch marks. Granted, they were the light-colored ones, but they were still there. I also had a C-section scar on my lower abdomen from when he was a stubborn ass and didn't wanna evacuate the womb. We waited, but in the end, he had to come out.

So I embraced that little pooch that would never be flat on my tummy, and even though I had to replace pants every year because my thighs would wear a hole where they rubbed together, I was happy with myself.

As soon as Jenson was done, he excused himself to go hang out in his room. I heard him turn on his video game and start chatting with his friends.

I sat at the table alone, and thought about what I was going to do now. My kid had reached a point where he didn't wanna hang out with me all the time. Which was nice, but I missed the time when he was my buddy and I was his. My phone dinged and I checked the message that popped up.

Which should I do? Dessert for dinner or cheese fries?-Period Buddy

"Oh my God, he didn't!" I groaned.

When did you get the chance to change your name on my phone?-Future Wife

"That bastard!" He put my signature as "Future Wife." Something was seriously wrong with him, like all of his marbles were just gone. I went into my settings and changed that immediately.

Aw, that's so sweet. You're finally realizing your role in all of this.-Joel.

I was about to text him back when Classic by MKTO started playing on my phone as a ringtone. It was the man himself, and I really shouldn't be surprised to see he changed the ringtone as well. Apparently he was a ninja at changing shit on my phone. Denied. I was not about to answer that.

Oh, that's cold. Only two rings!-Joel

Interesting choice of song.-Alessandra

It's my theme song for you. -Joel

Theme song? What the hell was that?

Theme song?-Alessandra

Theme Song= A song that would describe you/your feelings at the moment. -Joel

Classic was his theme song for me right now?

Those flutters in my stomach from earlier came back. I wasn't sure what to think about this one, because it was actually pretty damn swoon-worthy. How did he come up with something like that?

It's something my friend Killian and I used to do back in the day. Never stopped speaking in theme songs. What's yours right now?-Joel

Hm, if any song could describe me right now, what would it be? I thought about messing with him, but it felt like we were having a moment that was real. Not just playing around. Which made it harder. Honestly it took a few minutes for me to run through my mental playlists. I chewed on my lip as I typed out my text.

On My Mind, by Ellie Goulding -Alessandra

I went with honesty. I honestly wish I didn't have him on my mind. But I did.

I was thinking. I enjoy going out but don't always care to be hounded on by the paps. Take you up on that offer to help disguise me, then go out on a date? No expectations of sex. - Joel

Go on a date with Joel? I didn't know if I could do that.

God, I felt confused. I wanted to give it a shot, but I really was scared it would fuck up my life in some way. Whether it hurt Jenson, my job, or my heart.

"Hey, kiddo?" I called out to Jenson. I wanted to talk to him about it; maybe having his input would make me feel better.

"Yeah, Mom?" He came out of his room and waited for me to ask whatever question he knew was coming.

"Come sit with me; I have something to talk to you about."

He did, but looked nervous.

"What would you think if I went on a date with Joel?" I wasn't sure if he would be all about it or if he would wish I didn't. It could go either way.

"Joel Kline?"

"Yeah, kid, Joel Kline. He kinda asked me on a date. I'm not sure what to say. I won't do it if you don't want me to." One word from my kid, and I would never think twice about it again.

Chapter Eleven

Joel

Ok. -Alessandra

She said okay! To a date with me!

I jumped up from my bar stool and fisted the air like the kid in *The Breakfast Club*. Yes!

Now I just needed to come up with a date for us to go on. Something she would enjoy, where we could spend some time actually talking, get to know each other.

I racked my brain, and only had one idea in mind as I dug into my molten chocolate lava cake with ice cream that I picked up from a diner on the way home.

Alessandra seemed like the type of woman that would have fun in any situation, but my idea was going to be a winner for sure. It was the perfect first date. Time to talk, have fun, and let our worries go for a night. And when it was over, I would take her home. Hopefully score a hard-on creating kiss, with maybe a little squeeze of her ass, before I sent her on her way to bed, where she would then masturbate to thoughts of my kiss.

Oh, yeah. We would both get off thinking about that kiss before the night was over.

I tossed the plastic plate in the recycle bin, and sat on the couch with a smile on my face. Alessandra's face while she touched herself was the best I had in my spank bank right now. I would watch her rub her clit all day. She loved to screw with me, so of course she would be all into it. Moaning. Writhing.

And now I was hard.

I grabbed my phone and decided to test something.

Can we upgrade from period buddies to masturbating buddies? I think it would be mutually beneficial. -Joel

She would either take me seriously, or roll those sexy blue eyes of hers and move on. Most likely the latter, but for a few seconds before my little notification ringer went off I was hopeful.

Sorry, that audition already closed. The role was given to my bunny. -Alessandra

I fucking knew it! She did get off and take care of business!

Some women were weirded out by their own vaginas. I mean, if you didn't know how to pleasure yourself—know what you like—then how was the man you want to pleasure you supposed to know?

My hand went to my jeans and unbuttoned them, letting my dick spring free.

Was it wrong that I wanted to keep texting her, and let her fire get me there? Her attitude was the hottest thing to me. Never had that been the main attraction to a woman for me, until her. I wanted those claws on me, digging deep.

Instead of being a creep and one-sided sexting, I simply closed my mind and thought about her touching herself on the other end of my couch. She would be cruel enough to be so close to me, but of course would stop if I came any closer.

Her legs were spread wide, showing me her glistening cunt that was all wet from me. I would lick my lips in anticipation. Fuck, I bet she tasted fantastic. I wanted to dive at her core and drink her up. Those fingers would grip my hair, and I would grit my teeth from the intensity, but would carry on eating out my sweet girl's sex.

Bing.

My eyes opened and looked at my phone. Maybe she changed her mind?

Stop jacking off thinking about me.-Alessandra

Busted.

But really, did she think I was going to stop now? Yeah, right!

Shhhh. Just let it happen.-Joel

Gross. -Alessandra

And her fake disinterest was making me smile, and getting me hotter. My balls started to tighten. My release was getting close.

Too late now to play the good guy. She was involved in this, whether she knew it or not.

That ass though.-Joel

I will not be a part of this.-Alessandra

Too late.-Joel

I take it back, I'm not going on a date with you if you are really touching your dick right now.-Alessandra

She didn't mean it. God, I could see her face through this whole conversation. Her little eyebrow, raised with attitude. But then her eyes would get wide, seeing what I was doing. I wish I knew what she would do if she walked in on me right now. Would she join in, or find some way to torture me?

"Fuck!" Thinking about the things she would do made me peak. Cum shot out of my dick and flooded my hand. It was almost too much; I felt my vision go dark for a few seconds.

After cleaning up, I sent her a text and got ready for bed. Tomorrow was a long day, and then my date with my lovely lady would commence.

See you tomorrow. -Spent Joel

Night. -Spent Alessandra

I shook my head and turned off the lights.

The smile on my face never faded, even as I found sleep, where I met with my sexy Brazilian on a topless private beach. It was a fantastic dream.

The next day went by quickly, which was great for me. Alessandra did her job, and there was no flirting or talking about our new upgraded buddy system. Because let's face it, she really did get off like I did.

We were just too busy. The movie was coming along, and although we shot the scenes out of order, I could tell it was going to be one hell of an epic movie once everything was put together and had some music added to it.

I told Alessandra I'd pick her up from her house around 6:30 p.m. so she could put on my beard, and she agreed. She was still going on a date with me, and I knew it was my chance to keep proving myself to her that I wasn't this shithead actor that screwed everything in sight.

I was working harder than I ever had before to win a girl, a certifiable crazy girl, but she made it worth it. I was the Joker to her Harley Quinn. The romantic Suicide Squad version, not the comic book version. Those fuckers were horrible to each other.

As I drove back to the cottage to get my shit, I tried to come up with another movie couple analogy for us. Jack and Sally? No, too emo.

Leddy and Dom? Not bad-ass enough for that.

Edward and Bella? Definitely not.

I would figure it out eventually. Every couple had one. Maybe a food one. Mac to my cheese. But we were more than food. This was Hollywood, and a movie was what brought us together.

Chapter Twelve

Alessandra

He was going to be here any minute.

I looked around my house and hoped it looked okay to him. He said he lived in La Jolla, so I'm sure his kitchen was bigger than my whole apartment, but it was the best I could do. So if he wanted to date me, then he would see me as I was, including my small, two-bedroom, one-bath apartment.

Which was quiet, thanks to Jenson being over at his friend's house.

When I told him that Joel wanted to go on a date with me, he literally all but tossed me at the actor, saying I better not mess this up for him. He walked back to his room with stars in his eyes, probably hoping we would get married, and Joel would be his new dad. I swear he already told all his friends that his mom was going on a date with THE Joel Kline. The infamous, the hero, a friend to all the children in the land.

What was I thinking?

A knock on my door gave me no chance to come up with a reason to back out of my decision. He was already here, and there was no stopping him once he was in my space.

I opened the door and let him in.

"Welcome to mi casa," I said, arms spread wide.

Which he took as an invitation to hug me.

"Uhh." I felt sort of weird. Like I was ambushed by his arms, and I hadn't mentally prepared for it.

"You aren't Spanish," he commented as he pulled back and looked around.

"Bem-vindo à minha casa," I said, rolling my eyes.

"It's so sexy when you let the Brazilian out of you," he purred and I felt the tingles in my stomach. Okay, kids, time to move this along.

"All right, let's work on your awesome disguise so we can go to this mystery date you've planned." I held out my hand for the little storage case he had in his.

I gestured for him to follow me into the bathroom and sit down. He knew the drill.

"Nice place," he commented, but kept it short so I could put the adhesive on his chin and jaw. His jaw was really something. Very lick-worthy, if I let myself admit it.

"Thanks, it's close to the beach, which is important to us. We don't need a lot of space." But then a thought came to my head, and I changed that last bit.

"Well, another bathroom would be nice. Sharing with a teenage boy has gotten interesting." My poor eyes.

"Oh yeah?"

"Yeah, I caught him choking the chicken the other day. We were both mortified. I knew it was going to happen, but I didn't want to *see it.* I scrubbed the whole bathroom because all I could mentally seee was jizz everywhere." As I talked, I held out the fake beard and gently placed it in its proper positioning, patting gently to adhere it.

"Oh, the good old days. Shower time was my fun time. Used to piss my sisters off, how long I'd be in the bathroom doing my business." He smiled, and I just shook my head.

"Boys are gross." I started touching up around the edges of the beard to make it look authentic.

"Girls aren't any better." He shrugged and kept still for me.

"There. All done." I took a step back, and looked him over. A beard suited him well. He could pull it off, for sure. Kind of made me want to sit on his face, but I knew it wasn't real. And I would definitely not be doing that.

He stood up and looked in the mirror, running his fingers through the fake hair.

"Much better. At least with this and my hat, people won't realize it's me, and we can enjoy ourselves more." He looked at me, and I patted his back in support. We would see if people noticed him or not. The whole idea of a disguise was fun, in an undercover sort of way.

"I'm gonna go change real quick. Make yourself at home." I ushered him out of the bathroom and towards the sofa. When I turned to walk into my bedroom to change, I felt his presence behind me. My head moved back to see what he was doing.

"You said make yourself at home. If this was my home, I'd be following you to the bedroom. I would be more comfortable in there." I swear. This guy was something else.

"Sit." I pointed towards the couch, and he mocked a dog bark. That's right, who's my bitch? Instead of going to the couch, he went over to look at the pictures of my family on the wall.

Quickly, I changed into a pair of shorts, a cute blouse, and some ankle boots. I retouched my makeup with the mirror over my dresser, and pinned half of my hair up to give it a slightly tussled look. One last spritz of body glitter spray, and I was good to go. Feeling like one hot mama, I strutted out into the living room, ready to get this date rolling.

"Am I allowed to touch you at all?" Joel's voice was different than just before. Lower. Sexier. Can he touch me? I felt nervous about that. We'd been battling back and forth for two months now, and I didn't know what would happen if he touched me. Honesty. I would be honest with him about where I was at when it came to him. It was the only way we could move forward to whatever was happening.

I walked over to him and looked at the pictures on the wall. My favorite picture was one of me right after I had Jenson. He was so tiny, and I loved him something fierce. My hair was a mess, and I was wearing a shirt that had a wet mark on my breast from leaking milk. But the look in my eyes and his, as he looked up at me with his little fingers stretched up to touch my face, still made my heart swell.

"I was so young when I had him. Seventeen. He wasn't planned, but I loved him desperately." I smiled at the picture and turned to face Joel, who was watching me very intensely.

"His father was an aspiring actor. He left us for the chance to live the Hollywood life. We did fine. I wouldn't have it any other way. But he put on a good act, and I fell for it." My hand reached up to touch Joel's bearded face, and even though I'd done it hundreds of times before, this was real. I was under no influence of hormones, or my job. I was touching him because I wanted to.

"I'm nervous about letting this move with you. Be patient with me?" I asked, and he leaned into my hand. The gesture was sweet, and it made those butterflies flap away in my tummy. He didn't say anything, which for him was a first, but when he nodded that he understood, I felt like a weight had been lifted.

"Thank you. I can see there's more to you than what I assumed; I want to know more if you'll let me." He took a step back, away from my hand, making me look at him with a little confusion in my expression. Was he not okay with taking things slow?

"'Take Your Time,' by Sam Hunt." He gave me a smile, and I found myself wanting to hug him in thanks. This theme song thing was pretty cool, and kind of romantic, when used properly. I did like that song, and knew the lyrics. So I knew he just wanted to spend time with me, and was giving me what I wanted.

"Doesn't change that I wanna kiss the shit out of you right now. But I'll keep the suspense up and wait until the end of our date. Otherwise you won't wanna keep your lips off me." And there's that mouth of his!

Chapter Thirteen

Joel

I knew she'd like that one.

Her exasperated smile, and shaking of the head, didn't fool me.

"Shall we?" I held out my hand, hoping she would accept the gesture. She did. I mentally patted myself on the back for the little victory.

We walked out of her apartment after she locked the door, and then she laughed, seeing my truck.

"You're trying not to attract people's attention, but you pick me up in this?" I looked at my candy apple red 1954 Chevy truck that Killian delivered to me a few months ago.

"Lots of people have classic cars," I defended and opened the door for her. I was a gentleman sometimes, after all.

Money or no money, I always had a love of cars. Fast cars, unique cars, trucks, I liked them all. Now I was just able to collect them. I never let them sit in my big garage for too long, so it was this girl's turn to come out and play.

The drive over to our mystery date was easy. I didn't wanna come on strong so I asked her about simple things. Mostly her son. Mothers loved to talk about their kids. My mom would never shut up about her 3 spawns. I really like watching the way her face lit up when she talked about him, and as far as I can see, besides the normal teenage boy stuff, he was a really good kid.

Seemed cool when I chatted with him. I had no issues with kids at all. One day when I wanted to slow down from filming I would want my own. I figured a lot of women around thirty already were divorced or had a kid or two of their own, which I was fine with.

When we pulled in to the parking lot, I saw her eyes light up. She tried to hide her excitement. It was cute. I could see the young woman inside of her that she didn't really get to be, having a child so young.

"Ever been?" I hopped out of the truck and went to open her door. Honestly, I was a little surprised she waited for me to open it.

"Jenson had his tenth birthday party here."

I placed her hand in mine, and she didn't pull away. Together, like a normal couple, we walked together into The Zone. We were going to do it all: bowling, the ninja course, bumper boats, mini golf, the whole works. Our inner teenagers were going to come out tonight. It was the perfect way to get her walls down enough to see the woman she really was.

"What do you wanna do first?" I was leaving it all up to her.

"Maybe I should have had a margarita before this," she mumbled, seeing all the teens running around everywhere. There were some adults like us, too, on a date as well, so we weren't total creepers. I just looked at her, waiting for her choice.

"Um, let's do mini-golf. Warm up the fun before we do the heavy hitters." Mini-golf it was. I got us one round of eighteen holes and grabbed the little card and pencil. We both picked out our clubs, and balls. Hers was pink and mine was blue. I knew she was expecting a blue balls joke, and so I wouldn't disappoint her. To my credit, I only did one.

She went first, naturally, and I stared at her ass as she bent down to place the ball in its spot and lined her club up. Ass sticking out while she concentrated, it was very distracting for me.

She hit the little ball and it bounced around. She sucked, which made me snicker.

"Yeah, yeah." She walked down and tried again. Two more times then it finally went in the little hole.

"Let's see you do better." I kinda felt bad for the girl; there really wasn't much I wasn't good at. I was one of those people who were naturally good at most things, and the things I wasn't good at, I learned. Golf was a learned sport. When directors wanted to take you golfing because that's what they like to do, you learn to golf.

I bent over like her, shoving my own denim-clad ass out, which made her laugh. I lined up the club.

Hole in one.

She huffed and walked over to the next hole. After grabbing my ball, I wrote down our points and followed suit.

Six holes later she was all riled up and losing the game. The competitive side of her had come out, and I found it undeniably sexy.

I'd had a hard-on since she started cursing in Portuguese on hole three. But despite the added discomfort in my jeans, I was still whipping her ass, and she was not liking it. In a cute way.

"Here, let me help you, crazy." My arms wrapped around her and held the club with her hands.

"I'm going to pretend you don't have your dick on my ass in front of all these people," she whispered, and I chuckled.

"Whatever helps you sleep at night." I moved our hands together, and whispered encouraging words in her ear. I may or may not have also enjoyed the hell out of being so close to her, getting to hold her, smelling her hair. Classic move to get close, teaching her something.

"I know what you're doing," she hissed, all sassy.

"And boom!" We hit the ball and what do you know? She nailed it. She leapt out of my arms and did a little victory dance.

"Take that, sucker!" She wiggled, and I was mesmerized.

"You had a good teacher," I reminded her, to which she gave me the finger.

"Fine, fine. You had the magic dick touching you, giving you the power to put the ball in the hole. He's good at that, you know, *entering holes*." I walked over to the next spot and stood behind the couple in front of us, waiting for our turn. I could tell she was ready to spout out some comeback at me but held it in since there were other people so close.

She must have swallowed that retort of hers by the time we were alone again, because she just went to work and only missed the hole once. It was an improvement.

After mini-golf was finished, we moved on to something a little less skill-oriented: bumper boats. She was ready to sink my boat, and God did she try.

She had revenge in her eyes from losing to me, and I just ate it up. I'm sure she could do some damage if she wanted to, but this was just adorable, and I wanted to cuddle with her. Which was like trying to cuddle with a lioness. I was officially that stupid guy that wanted a lioness in his house to spoon. One day I was going to get my leg chomped off, and I didn't care one bit.

The more we bumped, the more her smile grew, and the harder and harder I fell. Because really, I think I knew from the first meeting that she wasn't a girl I would ever forget. I'd maybe gone through some steps to get her around me that I shouldn't have. But she was here now, and having fun. With me. Giving me the time of day, and a glimpse into who she was as a person. A fierce woman, who I wanted to immerse myself in and never come back up for air.

As I day dreamed about my lioness, she came at me good and I got splashed right on my crotch.

Chapter Fourteen

Alessandra

Dear God, Joel Kline had a big cock.

I'd felt it on my ass while he "helped" me play mini-golf, and now I saw it outlined in his wet jeans.

He was going to get arrested with that thing, being exposed like that around all these kids. I was genuinely concerned for him right now.

"Staring isn't helping, you know." His voice was lower, and I knew he was having a hard time trying to control it with me staring at it like it was a yummy corn dog at the state fair.

"Did you take a Viagra or something? I'm pretty sure it's been like an hour that you've been erect," I whispered to him as we moved to the next portion of our date. I suggested we try laser tag, because it was dark and he'd have to move around, hopefully helping his situation.

"Nope. All you, crazy. I'm starting to think we really are like Harley Quinn and Joker." He shook his head and we went into the room with the gear.

"Are you with me? Or against me?" He reached over to the two different color-coded chest armors. My mind was still on his hard-on, but I managed to answer him without too much delay.

"Against. Gotta lay the smackith down on your ass." I was feeling cool, and thought this would be fun. I'd played with Jenson before; he liked it. Of course, I wasn't thirteen like him, but I could still pull out my inner Charlie's Angels if I needed to. And right now, it was needed.

Joel smiled and suited up. I did the same, and he was just so sweet to help me get it over my head and boobs. A real gentleman, he was.

The instructor went over the rules and then separated us into two rooms.

When the light on the wall turned green, my blue team all ran into the blacklight-lit room and headed for cover. I went another way, hiding behind the columns to scope out the red team. I didn't see Joel but I had that sixth sense that he was around me. Slowly I crept around and then spotted some red.

Gotcha! I managed to get a few kids before one kid took me down. I had to wait fifteen seconds before my laser was ready to shoot again, so I tried to hide it out.

As soon as the blue light on my chest stopped blinking, I was good to go.

Then Joel found me. He got me square in the chest. I wasn't going to wait around so he could get me again, so I took off running, laughing and feeling like a teenager again.

We shot each other back and forth, and managed to get taken down by other kids in the room. I also didn't notice that there was a ramp in the room, so when I started going up and scanning for Joel, I felt like I was super-badass for managing to find him. But then that ramp started going down, and I fell to my knees.

Skidding down the ramp in true Charlie's Angels style, I held my gun out and shot Joel in my descent. The look on his face was priceless. I totally had rug burn on my knees from that move, and it was a total accident, but I turned it into a win for me.

When I stood up to try and compose myself a little, I was plastered against the wall and Joel's lips were crashing upon mine before I had time to blink.

The gun fell from my hand which went to his neck, lacing my fingers through his hair.

He kissed me like he had no other need in the world. It was purely primal. His tongue invaded my mouth, and I sought to match his passion.

This kiss was forever tattooed on my brain. I felt light, like a feather, as if his lips and my grip on his neck were the only thing keeping me tethered to the ground. But the more we explored each other's kiss, the more the burn began to escalate. I'd kissed him in a moment of weakness, driven by hormones. This was something entirely different, and I knew I'd never be able to come back from this moment.

The lights came on and the buzzer sounded, letting us know the game had ended, and we needed to leave the room.

"Get a room, guys," some teenager sneered at us and we parted our lips, just looking at each other.

"So much for slow." I smirked, but we both knew I had no problems whatsoever with that kiss.

"Your smile was so beautiful; I had no other choice." He leaned in and pressed one soft kiss to my lips before taking a step back.

We walked together in silence back to the room and took off our gear. We decided on bowling next; it would probably be the end to our night since we had to get up early for work tomorrow. We were past the years of wanting to stay up all night. We laughed, while we casually bowled, about how age changed us. We no longer wanted to get drunk and sleep until noon. Even when I tried to sleep in, I only made it to 8:00 a.m. I also didn't recover from getting drunk like I used to—a drink here and there was all I needed to feel content.

When our date was over, and Joel took me home, I debated seeing if he wanted to come inside and take things further, even though I said I wanted slow.

We reached the door and I turned to say something to him, but he pressed his lips to mine gently. It wasn't the type of kiss that led to wild sex against the door. It was the type of kiss that promised more.

"See you tomorrow," he murmured against my lips, the fake beard tickling my chin.

"Bye." I pressed my lips to his once more before we parted ways.

He waited inside the truck until I unlocked the door and walked inside. As I floated into my bedroom to shower and get ready for bed, I thought about all of the night's events. We still joked and carried on like normal, but there was a sweeter side to our dynamic. We had fun, we played, and we talked. It was like a teenage dream.

He made me feel like I was back in high school, no adult pressures lingering on my shoulders. Just a boy in my class, taking me on a date in his cool car, where we had fun, got to know each other, and fell into heavy "like."

When my head finally hit the pillow, I didn't let reality settle in about how things were different. Until the morning came, I would relish the feelings that he brought out of me, feelings that had been gone for so long. Having a baby, and a man who didn't want the responsibility, changed me. I wouldn't have it any other way, but it was nice to go back to that girl I was for a night.

Tomorrow would bring about a different scene between Joel and me. I still had to protect my heart, and my son. But I was letting go just a little bit to enjoy the moment. In this moment, Joel made me happy, and I was going to enjoy the feeling.

My alarm came early the next day.

I went through my normal morning routine, and when Joel finally came in the trailer, he said hello, but there was no morning kiss. We were professionals right now, making our jobs come first.

"I had fun. Thanks," I said, breaking the silence, and he smiled.

"We should keep doing it."

"I'd like that."

Kandi walked in shortly after I agreed and stole him away to get in his wardrobe. Things were going to be all right, just as long as no one figured out that we were testing the waters between us.

Chapter Fifteen

Alessandra

"I can't believe we are going to stay at Joel's house this weekend! You must be a really good lay, Mom."

Yep. That just happened. My thirteen-year-old son just commented that I must be a good lay in order to keep the interest of Joel Kline enough that he would invite us over to his house for the weekend. I didn't know whether to just smother him with the pillow, or walk away.

I went with option three. I always stressed honesty between us, and I would be honest with him now.

"Yep, might not want to put your food there without a plate, kiddo." He was going to need therapy one day because of me.

"Mom! Gross!" He looked at the kitchen table in disgust.

"Exactly. Don't say things like that about your mom and I won't put the picture in your head. Deal?" He nodded, a grimace still on his face.

"He asked me last week, before we went on our date, anyway." I put that out there. We actually hadn't done anything other than kiss a few times. Nothing life-altering like the kiss in the laser room, just pecks here and there. We were busy with the film, and I had to go to a school event for Jenson the past week. The end of the school year was in a month, so he had all kinds of projects and fairs that were happening. I was proud of him, and loved being a part of his school life.

Joel was not my top priority. He never would be, but that didn't mean I wasn't enjoying myself with him. Even just the little looks, touches, and our normal banter were a bright spot in my day.

"We will head there after school tomorrow, and you are going to be on your best behavior, got it?" I pointed my fork at him with a piece of shrimp still dangling.

"Yep." He ate his food, and I decided to bring up something I'd been thinking about for a while but didn't think I would be able to actually do. Thankfully, this job was helping to pay off some credit card debt that I racked up when things got tough.

"So, you know how I said you were going to be staying with Grandma and Grandpa while I worked away from home in a month?" He nodded and started chomping on a piece of garlic bread. It was gone in three bites.

"Well, I was thinking. If you are good for the rest of the year, and get an A in your history class, that before you go to stay with them, we can go swim at Monterey and do some of their special tours."

"No shit?" He jumped up and started celebrating.

"Mouth!" This kid, I swear.

"Sorry! Mom, that is awesome!"

"Well, it's not official yet. You still have to do good the rest of the year." I reminded him, and he shook his head yes. He promised over and over that he would be good.

Joel texted me around ten at night, just as I was getting ready for bed.

Are you ready for a weekend of debauchery and other fun activities?-Master of Your Universe

This guy. He must think he was something else, changing his name on my phone again. But joke was on him. Just before we left today, I changed his ringtone to something more fitting. Tomorrow I was going to call when he was around everyone, embarrassing him. Figuring out the password was easy when he does it in front of me all the time.

Oh yes, I was just telling Jenson that we were going to have sex in front of him so he could see how it was done.-Future Wife

Really? This again!!

You just had to take it to the next level. -Joel

Your question was dumb, it needed a dumb answer.-Alessandra

It really did.

I'm ready to have you close again. It's been a long week.-Joel

I didn't know what to say to him. I wanted that too, but after going the whole week without much time for touching, I gained some of my nervousness back when it came to him. No one at work knew we were sneaking quick kisses when we were alone for a minute. But in his own home, around my son, and Joel's friends? He most likely wouldn't stop touching me.

Was that weird to do around my son? I hadn't dated anyone since his father left us so long ago. Anytime I wanted a man, I left town and hooked up with a guy I met at a bar. But in reality, it had been a long time since I did that, even. Like years. I was a thirty-year-old spinster.

The night I met Joel I was trying to get back on the horse, and it turned into a disaster. So being with someone was weird to me.

We're going slow. No expectations this weekend.-Joel

It was like he was reading my mind. I was overthinking things and needed to hear that he was okay with my jitters.

See you tomorrow. ;) -Alessandra

He didn't reply, but I knew he was probably smiling like a goof, seeing my wink face. He would find something like that cute.

I left my phone on the nightstand and rolled over.

Hopefully this weekend wouldn't be a big mistake. But I guess there was only one way to find out.

I could tell Joel was excited for this weekend the whole day at work. He was on his "A" game while filming, and even though we had no time to talk, we said so much with just our eyes.

As soon as I was done with work, I drove home in my old Subaru Forester, and went to get Jenson. I threw our boards on the top, he had our bags all set to go, and we shut the house down.

He was on cloud nine as we drove in traffic down to La Jolla. The address Joel gave me was right by the water, where all the millionaires and above lived. He had been so down to earth with me since we met that I had forgotten that as a movie star, he was insanely wealthy. I never felt inferior to him, even in his shiny red truck. He was just Joel, the pain in my ass that I was sort-of dating.

"Almost there." I stared at all the walls and gorgeous houses as we drove down his street.

When we made it to the gate with his number on it, I was feeling those butterflies in full flight.

"I'm nervous," I admitted, looking at Jenson before buzzing Joel.

My sweet kid, with his scruffy-styled black hair and blue eyes, stared at me. He was my best friend. Even if I had to be the tough mom sometimes, we always had each other. He put his hand on my shoulder, and I thought he was going to tell me it was going to be okay. Because let's be real, there is no way he would tell me to turn the car around. Not when he was going to be spending the weekend with his idol. But I didn't expect him to sternly look me down and say,

"Chin up, buttercup. Time to nut up or shut up."

Chapter Sixteen

Joel

I watched Alessandra and her kid pull into my driveway and park. Killian and Livia were getting in later this evening, so it was just going to me, my girl, and the kid, until they arrived.

Dinner was in the oven, and the weather was great. I had a feeling this weekend was going to be pretty epic. Everyone I wanted in my life would be here, except my family, but I'd see them for Christmas, so I didn't sweat it.

Alessandra was throwing her mom attitude toward the kid when they got out of the car. I couldn't hear what they were saying, but I knew he must have said something inappropriate because she was going full "mom" on him.

Taking pity on the kid, I decided to walk out to them and help with their stuff.

"Welcome to mi casa." I winked at Alessandra when her head swung towards me.

"Sup." Jenson gave me the nod and started untying the boards that were on top of the car.

"Let me help you with that." I untied the other side, and we took the boards off together. They were decent, but I knew they deserved better. I wondered if Alessandra would be opposed to me getting them some new rocking boards. The more I thought on it, the answer was very clear: she would not be okay with that.

Maybe once we were official, I could sneak it on a birthday or something like that.

"Oh, man, can I see the cars?" Jenson's voice was slightly squeaky in his excitement. Poor kid, must still be going through puberty. Shitty time for all. He eyed my garage that was open to let the building air out a little.

"Let's get our stuff in the house first, and then we can get the grand tour." His mom shut him down for now, but that didn't stop him.

Their two small duffle bags and surf boards were in the house in record time.

My eyes watched as Alessandra took in my home. I wondered what she thought. Was it too much? Did she think I was this pompous asshole now, with my big house on the water and big garage?

"This place is huge," Jenson commented and walked over to the sliding glass doors that I had open to let the sea breeze come inside.

"Feels cozy," Alessandra commented, and with those two words my stressful thoughts were gone.

"Thanks, I had help with the decorating." I smiled, wishing I could totally take all the claim. Together we then walked up the stairs, and I showed them their rooms. Jenson wanted the room with a balcony looking over the water, and I put Alessandra close to my room. Purely by coincidence, of course.

I meant what I had said about no expectations. To be honest, having my friends plus her son in the house, I knew we weren't going to be alone, probably at all, during the whole weekend. But I was happy just being around her.

"So, kid, come here," I called out to Jenson, while his mom was putting her things away. It was time the kid and I had a little heart-to-heart.

"Ready to look at the cars?" I asked, and he nodded eagerly. I popped in to tell Alessandra that we were going to look at cars, and she said she'd be down in a minute. Perfect.

His face lit up when he saw my collection, and it was nice to share that enthusiasm with him. I loved my cars, and apparently, he did, too.

"So I wanted to talk to you, away from your mom, while I could. You good with that?" I wanted to make sure he was up for our discussion.

"Sure, what's up?" He came over and together we sat in my Ferrari to chat.

"I'm falling for your mom, kid. I'm taking my time with her because she needs it, and I'll wait. But I gotta know that you're all right with it. Me and her. You and I haven't really gotten the chance to talk much, but I'm a good guy. I'll treat her right, I'm—" He interrupted me before I could keep saying how great I am.

"I'm good with it. And I know you're a big movie star, but I've got that crazy blood that runs through Mom. You know the drill. You break her heart, I'll get you back some way. Got it?" Yep, Alessandra's son. No doubt there.

"You got it. So you'll be good if I kiss her in front of you this weekend?" He made a weird face then looked off into the garage.

"Take me for a ride in the T-REX, and I'll look the other way." Ah, a negotiator in the house. All right. Easy deal for me to make.

"Deal. And it starts right now." I gave him a wink and jumped out of the car, jogging towards a set of sexy lips that were calling my name.

"Hey. Whoa!" My lips collided with hers, and I wrapped my arms around her waist, lifting her feet off the ground.

"Jenson," she murmured, but didn't stop meshing her lips with mine.

"He's good; we made a deal." I kissed her sweet lips for a few more moments before pulling back to look at her face.

"So beautiful." I pushed the hair that was trying to cover her face back behind her ear. A blush coated her high cheekbones, and I smiled. Yes, this weekend was going to be epic.

"'Hooked on a Feeling' by Blue Swede." The twinkle in her eye made me say it. I was totally hooked on this girl.

She laughed and pushed me back, but I wasn't having that yet. Nope. I got to touch her, and hold her. I was going to do it as much as I could.

"Not in love with you, Cowboy Casanova," she teased, and while that may be true, I wasn't giving up hope that she would fall. She wouldn't go easy; I'd probably have to throw her off the cliff and into love.

Realistically, we are most likely talking about going straight-up Spartan, kicking her into realizing she is hopelessly head over heels for me. We were destined to be together. That was all there was. Her chest would recover from the kick later on.

"'It's Gonna Be Me,' by NSYNC?" I tried again, this song rang true as well. But she just laughed, and I couldn't help but kiss that smile I caused.

"You are something else." She shook her head sideways, and I knew she found me charming.

Jenson came over to us a few seconds later, and while she tried to pry herself away from me, I grabbed onto her hand and we walked back into the house together to check on dinner.

She and Jenson were setting the table while I grabbed the steak pinwheels out of the oven.

When I heard Alessandra humming the melody to "It's Gonna Be Me," I knew I had her. It was just a matter of time. I knew she was going to be mine in every definition of the word.

It was *so* going to be me.

Justin Timberlake would never let me down.

Chapter Seventeen

Alessandra

Dinner was really good. Of course, I was learning that there really weren't many things that Joel couldn't do. Which was both irritating and amazing.

I hated cooking, but I did it. Jenson knew he wasn't getting anything super fantastic when it came to my cooking, but he ate it like a trooper and carried on. We both loved it when Mom and Dad would come to visit and cook. My mom was a great cook.

After dinner was over, we went outside and hung out by the fire pit. Jenson went to the water and played around with a boogie board. Joel and I just sat there, watching him and enjoying the breeze.

"He's a good kid."

"Yeah, he can be a punk sometimes. But I love that little asshole." I thought about how he was growing up so fast.

"Ever thought of having kids?" I turned to look at Joel's face, curious. We were still getting to know each other. This was a normal question to ask someone of our age.

"Yep. Love those little assholes." He winked at me, and I wanted to roll my eyes, but didn't.

"You want anymore?" he asked, and I scoffed. The thought of having another kid was insane. But then again, I took care of Jenson pretty much by myself and it hadn't been easy, particularly given how young I was when I had him.

"Maybe, if I wasn't alone." I didn't want to see his face after my answer. Talking about Jenson's dad wasn't something I wanted to do right now. Joel didn't say anything, obviously getting that I didn't want to go into it. But it was still nice that he didn't push it.

We sat there together, holding hands, because Joel was not letting me be close without one body part touching. As soon as Jenson came back to sit around the fire and warm up, Joel's friends opened the slider and joined us.

I instantly recognized the tall man with the blond hair from the bar. He was there with Joel when we had our first encounter. He was a good-looking guy, but I wasn't drawn to him like I was to Joel.

When his cute little blonde girlfriend bounced over to give Joel a hug, I felt myself smiling along with her. She was like a little ray of sunshine. Then I recognized her as the woman in the picture that I saw online before. Hugging Joel on the beach. She was that petite blonde woman.

"Hiya. I'm Livia, Killian's girlfriend." She came in for a hug, and I hugged her back.

"I'm Alessandra." I gave no other indication of who I was, because I wasn't sure if I had a title. But Joel, being the sweet man he was, gave me one.

"She's my unofficial girlfriend and future wife." He leaned over to give me a kiss for show, and I turned my head so all he met was my cheek, which he still kissed anyway.

"Oh. Well, that is very exciting!" Then she turned around to ask Jenson his name, and he was blushing, but muttered his name. Aw… my little boy was getting all flustered around Livia. She was very pretty, so I would say he has good taste. She was just very taken.

Killian wrapped his arms around her and sat back in a chair with her in his lap. He said "hey" to all of us, but that was it.

We all chatted about fun adventures we had been on. Killian was a truck driver, and Livia was riding around with him while she was working on her graphic design business, which I thought was pretty cool.

She talked to me about books, and asked me if I was a reader. I shook my head. The look on her face when

I said I wasn't much of a reader—her expression was as if I'd told her I had cancer. She quickly launched into describing some of her favorites in different genres, until Killian reined her back in a little.

I wish I read more, but I was just too tired after working all day, and then taking care of Jenson. The last book I remember reading was Jenson's science book, because I wanted to help him with his homework and couldn't remember any of that shit from school.

Killian wasn't much of a talker, but I could see he was a good man. He was gentle with Livia, and he really cared for Joel. They were best friends to the max. A movie star and a trucker. A friendship like theirs surviving the fame game gave me hope.

Jenson enjoyed asking Killian tons of questions about where he's been and what cool things they had done on the road. Killian and Livia were living life to the fullest, and that was really beautiful. I liked to think I was living life as best as I could.

When we all called it a night, I felt like something in me had changed. If Joel was truly serious about trying to date me, I would let it happen. Yes, he was an actor, and I knew how well he could act. But I had faith that he was being real with me.

I kissed Jenson goodnight and then took a shower, getting ready for bed. Except I didn't go to my bed.

Instead, I acted like a teenager, sneaking into her boyfriend's room and praying she wouldn't get caught by her parents.

I really hoped Joel wasn't teasing me when he said that this was his bedroom door, otherwise this was going to be awkward.

I slid inside the door and closed it quietly.

When I turned around to look for Joel, I didn't have to go very far. He was standing about seven feet away from me, a towel wrapped around his waist.

Oh. My. God.

His chest, his abs, and that V.

Oh, man, this escalated quickly.

He didn't say anything; he just stood there looking at me, waiting to see what I was going to say. Or rather, what I was going to do.

What was I going to do? There were so many options. Whip the towel off and hop on? I could start slow; I think that had been my intention when I came in here. To kiss him, and actually try to open myself up to him. When I say open, I didn't mean my legs, but now I was feeling like that wasn't a bad idea.

Without the plan I came in here with, I decided to just be present in the moment. I walked over to him in my shorts pajama set like I was a vixen who knew what she was doing.

His eyes never left mine, and I really liked that.

Something about his gaze made me feel like he knew inside my soul.

When I was six inches away, my hands reached out to touch him. His skin was hot and soft from the shower. Every bump of his abs sent tingles up my arms and through all the nerve in my body. He was so strong. Part of me ached to follow the lines down to something harder that was trying to escape the towel, but I wanted to really enjoy this moment, and right now he was letting me be in control.

I honestly had no clue what type of man Joel would be, sexually. I knew it would be good, that I'd always known. Chemistry was never our problem. But was he a dominant type of man? Did he like his women to be in control? My lower lip went in between my teeth in anticipation. I was about to find out.

Instead of following the rabbit hole down to his growing cock, my hands went up to his neck and pulled his head towards mine. Our eyes never left each other's until the moment our lips met.

We started slow— teasing, tasting, but the more we tasted the more we wanted.

His hands went to my hips, bringing me flush against his hard-on. From then his fingers moved to my ass, gripping me, pulling me even closer.

My nails dug into his neck from the sheer need for him.

"Those nails," he growled in my mouth, and I felt a fire light inside me.

"You like them?" I did it again, and he moaned, nodding.

Joel Kline moaning was *everything* in life.

"Fuck yeah." He was getting more rushed, and vigorous.

"I said no expectations, though, are you sure?" He pulled back, just out of reach of my lips, giving me one last out. It only furthered my decision to really not let my own issues stop me in this.

Instead of answering him, I leaned in and licked his lips before latching onto his lower one, sucking, and my right hand moved down to touch his cock. Now he had my answer. We were adults, and I knew what I wanted. I wanted to play with him. I didn't care what we did, but right now I just needed something from him.

"So fucking mine," he swore and picked me up, tossing me on his large bed and covering my body with his. The fact that his towel stayed on during the movement was amazing. He really was good at everything. My legs wrapped around his pelvis, and he ground himself against me, making me bite whatever I could get on him to stop myself from screaming. He grunted from the pain, but it seemed to only spur him on more. He liked it, and I sure as hell didn't mind dishing it out. I tended to be the girl that scratched, who left bruises and bite marks everywhere. At least I was his makeup artist, and could cover any of these up if I needed to.

Every movement of his towel-covered cock was rubbing against my sex, and I felt like just that friction could get me there.

When his hands went to my breasts, kneading them sharply, and he pinched my nipples hard, I came.

It was so unexpected that I didn't have time to stifle the loud moan that flew from my mouth. He covered my lips with his to help muffle the sound, but I knew he didn't stop it all.

Chapter Eighteen

Joel

I was going to come so hard, and there wasn't anything to stop me. Alessandra was under me, writhing and moaning out from the mixture of pleasure from my dick rubbing against her sweet cunt and my grip on her nipples. It was too much. I'd wanted her for too long to hold myself back from letting go. It was like all my fantasies of her, but so much better. Undeniably better.

Like some teenager, I came right there in my towel, dry fucking her in my bed.

We bit each other's lips, and I tasted a tinge of blood mixed in with the mint of toothpaste. I was addicted. Her brand of crazy was all I ever wanted.

When we both finally came down from the unexpected pleasure, I rolled off of her, and tried to catch my breath.

What would actual sex be like with her? The thought had me shivering. It would be pure ecstasy. No doubt in my mind.

"I really hope I didn't wake anybody up. That was just so—" She was trying to find words, and I knew how she felt. I was still reeling from the experience.

"Unimaginable.

"And trust me; I've had many fantasies about you. Not even close."

It was the honest truth. I would never be able to go back to imagining her while I jacked off. Only the real Alessandra in front of me would do.

She smiled, and I leaned over to kiss that sweet smile. I loved her loco, but I loved her smile more.

"Don't let your mouth ruin this moment," she teased, and I kept kissing her, proving my mouth had many redeeming qualities.

We enjoyed our time for a few more minutes before she muttered that she should go. I didn't want her to; honestly, I was ready to move her straight into my room. Permanently. I wanted to wake up with her in my bed, and snuggle during the night.

But she gave me one last kiss and told me she'd see me in the morning. Bet her sweet bottom, she would. It took everything I had not to tie her to the bed to make her stay. I didn't have any bed bondage equipment or anything like that. But I had a shit-ton of ties. I could fasten them together and be creative.

She gave me a wink at the door and closed it behind her.

I walked into the bathroom to clean myself up and finally get dressed in sleep pants. Sleep didn't come quickly for me. All I could think about was Alessandra in my bed, and on fire from my touch. She was everything I had expected and everything I ever wanted.

When I finally passed out with a smile on my face and her scent on my sheets, I knew tomorrow was going to be a great day.

And it was.

I woke up before everyone and made banana pancakes, and even though I got a knowing look from Killian, it seemed like no one else had heard Alessandra or our little nighttime rendezvous. He was a light sleeper, so I guess I should have known. But whatever. I wore her loud moan on my skin, along with the scratches on my neck and scab on my lower lip, proudly.

Everyone enjoyed their lazy morning, and I told Jenson I would take him for a ride in the T-REX before we started surfing. His eyes lit up, and I knew it was the right call.

Livia and Killian just relaxed on the couch, while Alessandra got dressed in her bathing suit and headed for the beach. She lay out under the early morning sun, and I could see my beautiful Brazilian dig her toes in the sand before I left. She was a beach babe, and it was just another item added to the growing list of reasons why she was meant for me.

I even had to admit that Jenson was growing on me, too. We talked about school, sports, and I even got him to open up about girls. He had a crush, and it was cute.

When we got back I snuck out to pick my girl up from her toasty chair and kiss her silly before jumping into the cold ocean with her in my arms.

I needed her fire, and I sure as hell got it. She yelped and then tried to drown me. It was love, in its purest form.

Since we were already accustomed to the water temperature, everyone brought their boards out, and suited up. We stayed in our suits, since we were already in the water, and we surfed as a group.

I couldn't have asked for a better weekend with my people. That night, Alessandra and I were too wiped to do anything but sleep. Just before my eyes closed, I thought again about how I wished she was in bed with me.

The next day Killian and Livia had to head out early, but I knew I'd be seeing them soon. Knowing Killian as long as I had I could tell that he and Livia were something different. He wasn't going to waste time before asking her to marry him and making her his forever. I was happy for them.

Alessandra and Livia hit it off, as well, promising to text each other, and that my girl would try to read more. Livia tried to put on an "I'll kick your ass if you don't" face but she had no bite to her little puppy bark.

I didn't want the day to end, and when Alessandra and her kid loaded up her car, I felt like a part of me was being taken away. They belonged here. Jenson wasn't too thrilled, but he knew he had school, and life had to go on.

I kissed my girl goodbye.

And that was it. We didn't have any words of endearment, or banter. We would see each other tomorrow, and would most likely have to go on like this weekend never happened. We didn't really talk about where we were, and any titles that had formed. She was willing to let me in, and that was all I cared about right now. I had plenty of time to convince her that she was moving in, and going to become my wife. We would be a happy family. Kid and all.

Yep. I had time.

You can't have an epic love story like ours without a few little wrenches thrown in along the way. But I've found the Sandy to my Danny, so I'm in it for good. Damn this name thing was hard.

Chapter Nineteen

Alessandra

I woke refreshed from my weekend, and was ready to take on the work week. When Joel saw me, he looked around to see if we were alone in the trailer, then he picked me up, and crushed his lips to mine. I giggled at how excited he was to be free with me. He could touch me; he could kiss me. But we both knew there was an unspoken rule to be professional at work.

"You need to just move in with me." He pulled back and set me down. I shook my head at his ridiculousness.

"Sure." I played along.

"It's going to happen." He pulled me in close and nipped at my lip, revving my engine up at an improper time.

Before we could put space between us, Kandi walked in.

She popped her bubble and stood there for a minute, just taking in the sight before her: me in Joel's arms, intimate clench, which I untangled myself from as soon as I could with her staring at me.

"Knew you two were going to break one day. Fine line between love and hate, people." She turned around and went back to the wardrobe section, not caring that the main actor and his lead makeup artist were smooching. I didn't know what to think about that. Did that say something bad about me, that it was almost expected? That Joel Kline could have any woman he wanted, that it wasn't a big deal?

Joel sat in his seat, and I started my work, moving on from that awkward moment. But my brain never stopped. Doubt after doubt flooded my thoughts, and I couldn't reel it back in. We had something real. Didn't we?

He tried to get some words in while I worked, but I just shushed him and pretended to add more makeup on his lips to keep him from talking. He did need a slight repair from where we bit each other's lips hard, so I didn't truly need an excuse. But I would have used it, anyway.

If everyone found out that we were together, I would just look like some bimbo that fell for his charms, or worse, someone looking to use him to get ahead. I felt like an idiot. And somewhere inside me I knew that it just wasn't true, but being on set where the actor was king, and I was no one, I couldn't stop myself from going there.

Kandi came and got him as soon as I set my brush down. The look in his eyes said that we weren't done talking, but I was, for now.

My thoughts only got worse as the day continued. Watching him and Nineveh do their job well meant watching them cuddling, and talking about love, and it looked real.

When they had to film their first kissing scene, I had to leave. I knew what trying to open up to him would entail. I knew he had a job to do, and would have to kiss people. Or even have to pretend to have sex with women for a film. But I was feeling weak in this moment, and just couldn't do it. I left the area while they were lip locked and headed to the bathroom to try and get my act together.

I wasn't acting like the grown, strong woman that I was. And I hated that. Why was I doubting this with him? Why was I caring what people thought about me?

I sat there staring at myself in the mirror, with my hands on the little sink in the handicap-accessible stall, trying to figure out how to move past this. I decided I wanted to try with Joel. We had a great weekend together. He made me come on his bed, and kissed me like I was something special to him. Jenson adored him, and he wasn't shitty to my kid. I was just overreacting. The kiss was just part of the job. Kandi didn't give two shits about us; she was just calling us out on what she saw coming.

The door to the restroom opened, and I was glad to be hidden in this stall. No one could see my face and how crazy I was acting.

Then someone knocked on my stall.

"Someone's in here," I called out to the person. Seriously, I knew no one else was in here, there was still another toilet to pee in.

"Alessandra, let me in." Joel?

I turned and unlocked the door, only for him to barge in and pick me up, setting me on the sink with him between my legs. Holy shit, that was quick. What was happening right now?

"Joel, this is the ladies' room!" I whisper-yelled. I didn't add the "anyone could see us" part after my exclamation because he didn't look happy right now, and I knew that wouldn't go over well.

"And it's where my fucking woman is having a crazy moment in her head right now."

I opened my mouth to defend myself, but he shushed me with a kiss.

"You own my kiss," he groaned.

"I saw you leave when I had to kiss Nineveh. It's my job. She is nothing at all to me. Those lips don't drive me wild like yours. Yours drove me wild even before I tasted them."

He kissed me again then pulled back to continue speaking.

"I don't give a shit who knows about us, or what they think. I'm not saying it's going to be easy. And I understand your situation is a lot more delicate than mine. But I swear, I will tattoo it on my ass if I have to, so you'll finally get who owns me." His forehead touched mine, and I felt what he was saying deep inside me. I took a deep breath and went in search of those lips that owned me, too.

"I'm sorry. It's just new. I haven't done this, and you're just so much. And—" I tried to keep talking, but his hands moved over my body and his kiss was searing my soul, making me forget the doubts and bad thoughts I was having before. I could be strong. I could do it.

"Oh," I moaned, when things started to heat up. He was pressing his cock against me, and I knew where this could quickly lead.

"Not here. We can't." My panting voice sounded almost pained from the words. With reason.

He cursed, but didn't let me go.

"You good? We good?" he asked, and I nodded. I did feel better. If I started to go down this path again, I just needed to remember this moment. It was real. We were real.

"Good." He gave my ass a swat before he took a step back, but I guess he didn't consider that he was keeping me stable on the sink, and my ass fell into the bowl.

That had a motion sensor to run the water.

On my ass.

"OH MY GOD! SO COLD!"

I hopped off the sink so quickly I thought I was going to slip and bust my backside.

"And that's my cue to leave." Joel was making a quick escape, and I wanted to throttle him. My ass was soaked right down my crack. It looked like something tragic happened in my pants.

"Joel! I need help! I can't go out there like this." I quietly yelled at him to help me in this predicament. He put me in it, technically.

"Just say you had an accident." He was trying not to laugh.

"What am I, four? I'm an adult. We don't pee or poop ourselves." But God, that's what it looked like. He ran off, and I was stuck trying to dry my butt under the hand blower.

I decided I'd just stay there for however long it took, but then the door opened again, and Joel came back carrying a dress from wardrobe.

"Here, found you this. It was the only thing I could grab quickly." He handed the old-looking dress over, and the displeasure I felt for him evaporated.

"Thank you."

"Just call me the Superman to your Lois." He stood tall, with his hands on his hips like the superhero he thought he was.

"Yeah, I don't think so." I rolled my eyes and pushed him out of the stall so I could change and get back to work.

"Yeah, that doesn't work either," I heard him mutter as he left the bathroom.

Chapter Twenty

Joel

Crisis one was averted, and Alessandra seemed to be coming along when it came to us.

But I was going stir crazy for her, and things had to come to a head soon.

It had been three weeks since our moment in the bathroom, and I hadn't gotten any real alone time with her since. Filming had been intense, and when we weren't filming, I had meetings with the studio about my next movie in the comic book series. This one was going to be a crossover with another, and the script was insane. We were talking a multimillion-dollar film.

Alessandra was busy with Jenson, who was in his last month of school, and getting ready to take him to her parents' house in Brazil. From there she would fly back here, and leave the next morning for Kauai.

Anytime that was not being occupied by filming, I was going to spend with her. I was like an addict going through withdrawals. One month in paradise together, and I was going to make it my own version of heaven.

I had finished my intense workout and headed for the shower when my phone rang.

Mandy Moore's "Candy" blared from my living room.

That woman. She had been changing my ringtone to songs she thought were embarrassing, or even her theme song for me at the time. And I did the same. I never bothered to change my password, because it was cute. Our fun way of screwing with each other, and I knew she liked it, too. So we kept up the fun.

"This better be a sexy phone call because I am going out of my mind over here." Yeah, I answered the phone like that.

"Oh, Joel, I'm touching myself right now," she moaned on the other end, and I found myself growing hard.

"Don't tease me, Lips. I've been hard for you for too long. You need to give up the goods soon, or I'm going to combust," I whined, which made her laugh.

"Feeling a little blue over there, Kline?"

"Yes. I need your P on my D very soon. We've been together for over a month! I feel like I've earned some coitus gratificationus." I totally made that word up, but whatever. I was feeling desperate.

"I know; I've been craving some Vitamin D myself," she admitted, and it made me feel worse. I so wanted to give her that healthy dose of D.

"But we will have time in Hawaii to have fun. No interruptions, besides work. I'll let you play hide the snake in the bushes."

"We both know you take your Brazilian heritage seriously down there; no bushes to hide in," I retorted, and I honestly had no clue if that sentence was true. I hadn't even touched or seen her vagina! I was all for waiting, but Christ. All we've done is make out and dry fuck each other, once! We were adults, and this was like torture.

"Nope. I'm more of a retro girl."

"Doesn't matter. I'll go la freak on your sweet mound no matter if it's jungle or beach." I was officially losing it. What the hell was I even saying. La freak? I needed medication.

Instead of thinking more on how insane I was feeling, I listened to her laugh, a sound that made me smile instantly.

"Okay, I was just calling to let you know I won't be able to hang out with you tomorrow before you leave. I promised Jenson I would take him to Monterey Aquarium to do fun tours and such, if he was good for the last month. And he was. So I will just see you in Kauai."

I wanted to groan with disappointment, that I wouldn't see her for four more days, but her son came first. And that was more than okay with me.

"No worries. I'll have plenty of time to iron out my epic proposal in paradise for you then," I joked with her and she laughed, like she always did when I talked about marrying her, or moving her in with me. I just smiled and thought to myself...all in good time.

She couldn't talk much longer, so I wished her luck, and told her to text me while she travelled. I knew she was going to be exhausted from running around so much. I had already booked her a spa day once she arrived and got settled. I thought she would like that, and I'm a thoughtful guy.

After we hung up, I went ahead with my plan to shower, and passed out. During filming, I never had much energy for anything but the job, working out, and sleeping. At least Alessandra understood that and didn't seem to have any issues with the grueling schedules. She liked her space, and it was a good trait for someone to have when being with me.

She could do it. Alessandra could handle everything.

A little nagging thought in my head knew there was still a little skeleton in my closet that she would not be good with, but I ignored it. She would fall in love with me, and it wouldn't matter. I have never been acting with her, and I have wanted her since that moment I saw her. She was it for me.

The Leia to my Han.

I actually got to sleep in the next day, since my flight wasn't leaving until noon. But since I woke up early every day, I still woke up at 8:00 a.m. I did a quick run on the beach, showered, and finished packing. I knew L.A.X. would be busy, so I decided to get there earlier than I was told by Leighton. Which was a good decision. Traffic sucked, and the airport was chaotic. I pulled my hat low so no one would add to my time, but a few people had stopped me to take pictures. It wasn't long before I had people gathering in clumps around me, using their phones to take pictures and video of me walking and getting a coffee.

It never bothered me, but I could see how Alessandra would be uncomfortable. I was used to it, but she wasn't.

I was able to sneak into the airline's VIP lounge and pretty much everyone in there left me alone. One older lady who clearly wasn't much of a movie fan sat next to me, and chatted about how she was traveling to Hawaii to look at the birds. Silently I prayed that she wasn't assigned to sit next to me. It was a long flight to sit and talk about the different breeds of birds in Hawaii.

Thankfully, the flight wasn't that full, and I had space next to me in first class. I shot Alessandra a text saying I was about to take off, and she sent me a picture of herself and Jenson in wet suits by the top of the big fish tank. I bet they were having a blast, and a big part of me wished I was there with them, enjoying the smiles on their faces. I would have liked to see Jenson get excited for all the sharks and fish. He really enjoyed everything ocean, which was so cool.

I spent the flight going over my lines, and read the script for the rest of the scenes we were shooting. They were going to be pretty intense, and a lot more scenes with Nineveh.

Which, hopefully Alessandra wouldn't have any more loco moments, seeing me with my coworker. Nineveh was beautiful, sure. And she was very nice, and quiet. A professional.

She was nothing like Alessandra. That woman could burn a building just by looking at it, if it bothered her.

When I landed in Kauai, I drove my rented Jeep to the beach house I rented near the set, and beelined for the water.

Chapter Twenty-One

Alessandra

I was dead tired. The past few days had been nothing but exhausting. Jenson had a blast at Monterey. We swam in their big tank, and went on all the behind-the-scenes tours. He got to watch the fish and sharks in a feeding frenzy, which was a little crazy to see but he loved it. I just envisioned myself in there being torn apart by the fish, so I wasn't all grins like he was.

Then we flew together to drop him off with my parents in Rio de Janeiro. They were thrilled to see us, and couldn't wait to start doing things with their only grandbaby. Jenson was going to have a really busy month. My parents weren't ones to stay in the house all the time—they loved to hike, swim, and even surf. We were outdoorsy people, after all.

As soon as I made it to Brazil, I had to turn around to head home, gather all my things for Hawaii, and get to the airport in a few hours for the flight to Kauai.

I'm sure Joel had a comfy seat in first class, and no one sitting next to him.

I was snuggled in between a large man and a young woman.

Whether he was okay with it, or I just looked like the walking dead, the man next to me didn't make a peep about me resting my head on him accidentally for a while.

When I finally made it to Hawaii, I found my two large suitcases easily marveling at the open-air baggage claim that took advantage of the beautiful scenery and tropical breezes.

"Welcome to paradise, Lips." I yawned and looked at Joel, too tired to ask him what he was doing here. Obviously, he was here for me.

Not caring if anyone was watching or had cameras pointed at him, I walked over and wrapped my arms around his waist. I needed to be held, or carried.

"Miss me that much, huh? It's okay, we have a whole month of fun and adventure together." His strong arms circled me, and I smiled against his warm chest.

"Sleep first," I mumbled, and he pulled back to grab my suitcases and carried them to a blue Jeep just a few yards away.

"You're taking me to the hotel?"

"Nope, you're staying with me in a house I rented near set. And before you fight me on it, I bribed Kandi with a year's subscription to the Bubble Gum Box to still say you are rooming with her. I doubt anyone is going to care."

He had taken care of everything, and I was too tired to fight him. I hopped up into the Jeep and he headed toward the love shack he rented for us.

After just a few minutes' drive on a winding, two-lane road, he turned off and drove up a long dirt driveway. This house was definitely secluded, I'd give him that.

When the little red bungalow with a wrap-around porch came into view, I was truly stunned. It was beautiful.

"Wow!" I took in the scenery before me and felt like it was something out of a fairy tale. The little house was nestled in lush green flora, and you could see the water on the other side of it. The mountains were behind us, so no matter where you sat on the porch, you would have a spectacular view.

When he parked the Jeep, I just sat there, staring.

"It's really beautiful." I opened the door, but he was suddenly there to help me get out.

"I thought you'd like it." He smiled, and I left my bags behind, wanting to go inside and explore. There was a table for four on the porch, and I smiled, thinking that it would be a nice place to have dinner.

The inside of the house was so beautifully decorated that it could have been in a magazine. I really wouldn't doubt that it had, at some point.

It had wooden walls, and pretty bamboo counters. The furniture was brown and off-white, and it flowed nicely with all the wood.

I walked over to the sliding glass door that was open to the sea and could have just died by the sight. I loved the water so much, and that pretty deep blue mixed with light green was my favorite view.

On the back half of the porch there was a large hammock that would be perfect for relaxing and listening to the sounds of the waves. Directly across from the hammock was a large claw tub. I guess with all the privacy this place provided, you could take a nice bubble bath outside without being exposed. I'd be down for that, too.

Continuing my tour of the house, I found out it had two bedrooms, two bathrooms, and was without a doubt the nicest house I'd ever been inside, aside from Joel's house in La Jolla.

"Wanna eat some lunch?" He pulled out a bowl of fruit from the kitchen and set it on the table. Technically it was a little after noon here, and I'd been on a plane for over six hours, but I needed that nap.

"I'm going to go pass out for two hours and then I'll be good for a little while." I walked over to give him a proper kiss, which he returned before picking me up gently and carrying me to the room. He laid me down in the big bed, which I'm sure we would be sharing for the duration of our stay. He wasn't going to let me sleep in the other room while he was in here, and I honestly didn't want to, either.

He took off my shoes, setting them on the floor by the closet, and then did the same for his shoes.

I watched as he climbed into bed. He was paying so much attention to me, and I was feeling all warm and fuzzy on the inside. I moved closer, and he put his arm around my shoulders so I could snuggle his nook.

Together we napped, wrapped up in each other like vines.

That two hours flashed by and soon he was failing at trying to wake me up.

"No wonder you don't ever want to have a sleepover; your breath smells in just two hours. I'd probably pass out breathing it in the morning."

So charming. Really, how was I not in love with him already?

"Go away!" I huffed air at him like a fire-breathing dragon, hoping he was telling the truth and it would scare him off.

"I was just teasing. You look like a beautiful goddess, waking from a peaceful sleep in the arms of her lover." He was teasing me yet again. I tried to roll over but he held onto me and brought me back to his chest. This time his lips were on mine, trying to wake me with a kiss.

It was working.

"Okay, you win." His teeth nipped at my lip and then it was on. My hands went to his hair, and the kiss deepened. Instead of trying to roll away from him, my legs wrapped around his hips, and I felt his hard cock against me once again.

"Think maybe we can get to third base this time around?" he muttered, and I wanted to laugh. God, we were acting like teenagers.

One hand went to my breast and the other to the button of my jeans. Yes!

"Shirt off," I commanded, and he whipped it off in seconds. My fingers went to his chest, needing to feel his skin against mine.

"I'm going to touch what's mine, Alessandra." His low, raspy voice made my whole body shiver. I wanted what was coming. Me.

His fingers found their mark, and he wasted no time coaxing me to opening up wide for him.

I moaned and writhed against him as he pressed his thumb against my clit, and one finger teased me before diving in. My back arched; it'd been so long since I'd been touched by a man.

His thumb was rubbing my clit, over and over, making me squirm.
"Fuck, you are so sexy. You love my finger fucking you… I'm going to give you another." He did.

"And another."

I cried out from the feel of his three fingers inside me, stretching me.

"And another, until you are stretched enough to handle my cock." His fingers that were on my breast gripped, and pinched my nipple through my bra. Oh, yes. He knew how to play me like he was my very own maestro.

"Joel," I whined, needed more. His fingers started pumping in and out, faster and faster.

"Fuck!" My nails bit into the skin of his chest before letting go and holding onto his shoulder.

Then his fingers were gone. My eyes widened, and I swear, if looks could kill, he would be dead right now.

His hands gripped the tops of my jeans and panties together, and pulled them down in one swift move.

"Show me your cunt, Alessandra." He looked so provocative as he stared at my bared sex.

"I just knew you were true to your heritage." He winked, and I swear he lunged for my sex, tongue entering me with a wiggle, and then sucking on my clit.

"My best fantasy could never touch real life. You are perfect," he mumbled against me, and the vibrations almost caused me to jump off the bed.

I was getting close, especially once he added a few fingers inside me. Without the restriction of my jeans, he could move more freely, pumping harder than before. When his teeth lightly bit my clit, I was a goner. My hands went to his hair and gripped him for dear life.

I cursed, unable to stop the flow of words, and I don't even know if what I said was in English or Portuguese.

My whole body tensed, and I rode every shudder of the orgasm that shot through my body.

I always said Joel's mouth ruined everything.

Well, it was official.

His mouth had ruined my vagina for all other men.

Chapter Twenty-Two

Joel

"The Man" by Aloe Blacc was running through my head as soon as her screaming calmed to gentle whimpers.

"While you lie there in orgasmic bliss, I need to do this."

I may be a complete asshole for doing it, but the desire was too great. I had no choice. Reaching over and grabbing my phone, I found what I was looking for, and pushed the button.

"The Man" started playing through the speakers, and I couldn't help but feel complete pride in myself. I was *the fucking man* right now.

The smile that hit Alessandra's face hearing the song and watching me was added to the list of why she was perfect to me. Some women would honestly think I was a douche for doing something like this at this moment, but she got me. She fucking got me.

"You're a dumbass!" she laughed, and I started to do a little dance for her amusement. She got an earth-shattering orgasm, and a sexy dance.

She was one lucky woman.

She laughed at me, and I ate that shit up. I moved my legs over her stomach and channeled the role of Magic Mike. I almost took a spot in that movie, but it conflicted with another one I was doing. I still had the moves though.

I grabbed her hands and ran them down my abs, rubbing them on my hard-on. She laughed, and when I brought my lips to hers, that smile never wavered.

The song ended, and I was quick to turn the player off before another song came on.

"You're lucky you're good at doing work."

I was too busy thinking about her use of words of me doing work on her cunt to realize that I was no longer in control of rubbing her hand against me—she was.

"My turn."

She straight up wrapped her leg around mine and surprised the shit out of me by rolling us over.

Her hands had my fly down and my dick out before I could blink. Girl had skills.

Just when her mouth was heading towards my dick and her eyes were looking up with a glint, I panicked.

"Wait!" My heart was beating erratically, and call it post-traumatic stress or just straight-up stupidity, but I couldn't get the vision out of my head of her biting my dick like she did that carrot.

She sat up and looked at me in confusion. Yeah, you and me both, sweetheart.

"Can you, um, start slow, and maybe like play nice with him first?" Yeah, feeling like *the man* was gone. I swear she blinked at me ten times in the past ten seconds.

"Uh, sure, everything all right?" She was concerned now, and that was not what I wanted.

"I've been a little traumatized, thinking about your mouth on my dick ever since you teased me and bit the shit out of the carrot."

She stared at me for a few more seconds before busting out laughing, collapsing on top of me.

"I'm serious! I haven't even been able to jack off to the thought of it. All I see is you taking a big chunk out of my dick!" I was so serious, it really has been awful.

"Okay, loco. Just relax and let me make that traumatic thought into a positive one." She finally stopped laughing and wrapped her fingers around my shaft. Slowly she moved up and down, and I started to relax, trusting her and trying not to let that stupid image invade my brain again.

I watched her lick her lips while staring at her hand moving, and that helped, too.

When she leaned down and flicked her tongue at my head, I knew I would survive.

As she continued to sweetly initiate oral with my dick, I found my body becoming fluid.

Once she saw I was relaxed, she let the crazy back out of the box and went to town on my cock.

"Fuck!" My hand went to her hair, and I held on as she sucked me like she was trying to pull my damn soul out of my body. Her tongue swirled and then pressed against the underside of my head, causing my abs to tense, and then shudder.

"Fuck my mouth, Joel," she demanded. Who was I to deprive the lady from what she wanted? With my fingers curled in her hair, I lifted my hips up and fucked her sweet mouth. She opened up and handled me. When I heard her gag a little, I tried to pull back, but she grabbed my ass and pushed me in further.

I cursed out a slew of words, none of them probably making sense. She dug her fingernails into my ass then sat up slightly, so I automatically stopped moving.

She jacked me almost torturously slow, before going back for more with her mouth—down so slowly, then back up, dragging her lips along every nerve.

Suddenly her pace quickened, and I felt like I didn't know which way was up.

Two more times she slowed down, then went faster, and I couldn't hold on any longer.

"I'm gonna come; if you don't want it in your mouth, tell me now." Ever the gentleman, I gave her the out of taking it all in her mouth.

"This time in my mouth, next on my tits. Deal?" she muttered, and that was all it took. Cum shot out and coated her throat. She swallowed everything, and all I could do was groan about how she was a dick-sucking goddess.

That carrot can go fuck itself; I had a new image to think about when it came to her lips on my dick.

When the final spasms subsided I just lay there, completely spent.

"I'll do whatever you want next time, as long as there is definitely a next time," I told her, and she gave my sensitive cock a kiss on the tip one last time before coming up and resting her head on my chest.

Life was perfect at the moment, even after we got up, and dressed again.

Alessandra wanted to go out to the water and take a walk before dinner, which I planned to have out on the porch with some tiki torches I found in the shed just by the house.

Together we walked hand-in-hand along the water's edge, just like every postcard of a romantic vacation from Hawaii. It was just too damn perfect not to do it.

She'd never been to any of the Hawaiian Islands, so she was happy as hell just to be experiencing it for herself. Only thing that would have made it all flawless for her would have been Jenson being here, too. As much as she enjoyed having time away from him, she still wanted him around, seeing him experiencing things and making memories together. I kissed the start of a frown away from her lips when she started thinking about how much she missed him, all while coming up with a plan that might change that frown upside down.

I made us dinner, and we watched the sun go under the water's line before settling down on the porch, watching the stars pop out.

We talked about things that we could do when we weren't filming, and while sexing her up was my first thought, I knew she would probably want to get out and explore the island. I would just have to sex her against a coconut tree here and there. Or maybe some waterfall sex. That was adventurous.

She went to take a shower after our dinner was eaten, and I had to make a few phone calls. I would have rather joined her, but duty called.

I sat in the hammock and listened to the waves lap against the sand. When she came out of the house to join me, we snuggled in the large hammock, both fell asleep in paradise.

Juliet and her Romeo.

Or maybe not. I'd prefer us both alive at the end of our story.

Chapter Twenty-Three

Alessandra

"Wake up, Lips, you've got a busy day ahead of you," Joel's voice called out from somewhere inside the house.

My eyes slowly opened, and I had to peek over a blanket that was covering half my face.

At some point, Joel left the hammock we were lying in together, and covered me with a blanket so I wouldn't get chilled. Instead of jumping out of the hammock, I tucked the blanket around my neck and simply listened to the waves. The gentle breeze moved the hammock back and forth in a sweet, rhythmic motion. How was I supposed to ever leave this spot?

"Nice bed head." Joel came walking out of the bungalow wearing just swim trunks, and I couldn't help but gawk at him from my blanket cocoon.

"Scoot over." He sat two plates on the wooden porch rail before somehow finding room in the hammock with me. He reached over to grab the plates and sat one in my lap.

"Pancakes." The last time he made pancakes they were exquisite.

"Banana pancakes." He winked and cut into his own set of them on his plate. Just looking at them made my mouth water. My arms shot out of the blanket like daisies in the spring, and I took a bite of those sweet cakes.

I moaned and complimented him on his cooking skills.

As soon as I was finished, I snuggled myself in the blanket again and let out a nice sigh of contentment.

"Don't get too comfy. You have an appointment to keep." He grabbed our plates and set them on the porch rail again.

"What appointment?" I asked, as he gripped my arms and pulled me over to his side of the hammock. Luckily neither of us fell out.

"A surprise appointment." He waggled his eyebrows and I rolled my eyes in response.

"I just wanna stay here all day," I whined. I meant that in two ways: here at the beautiful house on the water, and with him. Yesterday was a victory in his battle agenda. It was beautiful, and a day I would never forget.

Even though the need for sex was prominent after such a slow start to our relationship, we were enjoying each other's company. I'd never been with someone with whom I could laugh and use my wit. Even when things were heated, there was still fun in the air. We could laugh, tease, and be intimate all in the same moment. It was something I'd never experienced before, and that' showed me this was something different. Joel was trying to win my heart, and he was succeeding.

It wasn't long before he was kicking me out of the hammock and insisting that I get ready for my surprise. I was both excited and nervous as he drove us back to civilization, and then towards a fancy-looking resort.

"You've had a taste of my pussy and now you're dropping me off at a hotel?" I questioned him, and he laughed.

"Yeah, it was so nasty I can't have you around me anymore. We are over, Alessandra." He helped me out of the Jeep and led me through the lobby of the extravagant hotel.

"Okay, seriously, what are we doing here?" I was letting my impatience show.

"This!" He gestured towards two big glass doors with opaque glass.

"Ka Hoola Wai?" What does that mean?

We opened the doors and a beautiful spa was revealed.

"You're getting a spa day. Figured you needed some pampering after all the traveling you did. Plus, I'm guessing it's been a long time since you've done something like this." He held his hand out for me and once I placed it in his much larger one, he kissed my knuckles, nuzzling my hand against his cheek.

A spa day.

I'd never had one. There was never time nor money.

"All right, ladies, take care of my woman. Make sure you buff those devil horns on her head nice and good." He gave me a quick kiss before I could bite him and then he left.

I was then surrounded by women and escorted to a back room, where I was asked to undress and then wrapped up in one of the softest robes I had ever felt.

Hours later, I had been massaged, had a facial and seaweed wrap, and gotten a mani-pedi. I was going to owe Joel a spectacular blowjob for this. Weakness was not something I liked showing, and I needed this more than he knew. I was so tired, and run down. Years of doing everything by myself had taken its toll on me mentally, and it was nice to officially let go and just enjoy myself, to do what I wanted without thinking about how it would affect my child, my job or my bank account.

Joel met me at the curb when I texted him that I was all done and ready to be picked up.

"Feeling relaxed?" he asked whenI hopped in the Jeep.

"Yeah, except I still have this pain in my ass right now."

"Too much anal play? I told them to be gentle with the happy endings." He always had something to come back with,something I really liked about him.

"Yep, my ass is nice and open, ready for the threesome we are having tonight." I did not let my mind wander where my mouth went. There was no way in hell I would ever let two dicks near me at the same time.

"No can do, Lips. You and I are having a twosome tonight. Just your P and my D."

He drove us back to the house, and I told him I would make us some lunch, which was chicken quesadillas.

I was pretty good with a skillet, but that was about it. Briefly, I thought about just eating fruit and peanut butter and jelly sandwiches, but he had been making extraordinary meals for me, so I could try for him. When he bit into them and moaned, I knew I'd done all right.

"You ready to get back to work tomorrow?" I asked him, curious if he was ready for the hard work and long hours to continue. He nodded, but didn't speak with his mouth full of food.

"So far it seems like it's going to be a really good movie. I might even have to go see it in the theater." I took a bite of my food and mentally replayed what all had been filmed as of now. The movie was really going to kill it on screen.

"You should come with me to the premiere." He asked like it was no big deal, but it was. I was all for being with him now, but coming out to everyone? Still a pansy when it came to that.

"I don't know." My stomach was starting to turn sour; we were having such a good time. I didn't want to make him unhappy with my reservations about being out in the open with him.

He set his food down and looked at me with his head tilted to the side. Those blue eyes were looking at me intently, trying to figure my thoughts out.

"You don't think you'll be comfortable being seen with me by the premiere? A year away?" Shit, I did hurt his feelings.

"I just don't know. I really like being with you. You make me feel things I haven't felt before, but it's not just me, Joel. I have to take into consideration what your fame could do to Jenson. To our family. Things are just a little more complicated with you being who you are. Always in the paper, and on TV. And we don't know where our relationship will be then."

It was the pure, honest truth. I could handle it all, but what happened when the papers constantly published lies about Joel and me? Or worse, even included Jenson? My stomach dropped, just thinking about that. It could cause issues with school, and our relationship. Fame always had a price.

"I get it. But you don't." He looked like he'd bitten into a bitter apple, and abruptly stood, pushing his plate away. NO!

"I'm going for a walk." He walked out of the house without another word. I stared at the space on the porch where he had been before vanishing from my sight. I fucked up. He'd done all these sweet things for me and had been treating me like his princess, and I screwed it up with my mouth.

But what I felt was legitimate. My concerns were real, and I couldn't just blink them away. There was a reason that so many couples in the movie business never lasted, and the kids were usually the first to suffer from it. Always in the public eye, and scrutinized.

I pushed my plate away from me and buried my head in my hands. Tears assaulted my eyes, and I felt like such a horrible person. We were complicated. But I wanted Joel. No, I needed Joel. He was becoming such an important part of my life, and I wasn't willing to let him go. I knew it was wrong of me to keep yo-yoing him around, but I just wanted my cake and to eat it, too.

But sooner or later, I was going to have to choose.

Chapter Twenty-Four

Joel

"With you being who you are."

I churned those words over in my head for the rest of the day. A part of me felt bad that I had left her until the sun had met the sea, but I just hadn't been ready to go back yet.

I'd been thinking of the long-term game with Alessandra. Hell, I'd even thought the same sentence it in my own head before, but I didn't take into account all she said. I knew she didn't want to be in the limelight. Sometimes I didn't either, but I thought with some time that she would just ignore it, and everything would be fine.

Her having a family changed things in a way I hadn't considered. I'd seen firsthand how ugly things got for families that were in the movie business. Friends and coworkers of mine had their life destroyed because it was just too hard; it hurt their spouse and their kids.

It was selfish of me to ask that of her. But I wanted her too badly to walk away. The thought made me want to fall to my knees, all of my body being weighed down by the fear of losing what we had gained and what I knew we could have.

Jenson was a cool kid, and he deserved the best in life. I wanted to give it to him. Shit, I wanted his mom so much that I wanted him, too. I wanted them both.

But how much was too much for them to sacrifice for love? For me?

I was head over heels, madly in love with Alessandra.

I didn't need months to figure it out. I was falling before we had gotten to this point, and the past twenty-four hours solidified it. She was my woman, through and through.

Which made my head hurt, thinking about what to do. Keep everything a secret and hope shit didn't blow up in our faces?

Let her go?

There didn't seem to be any other options in my head, but there had to be, right?

I finally made it back to the house when the moon was high, and I knew I'd have some groveling to do after leaving her like that and not coming back till late. But I would do what I had to.

She was mine, and I'd go to the end of the universe for her.

We were like Lana and Luc from the film. I was literally fighting tooth and nail to reach her, and all I needed was her love to free me. I'd wait forever if I had to, but she was the only one for me.

I walked in the house, my whole body tense, ready for a fight. But she didn't come at me.

She wasn't in any of the rooms, and a sinking feeling in my gut led me to believe she'd left. My hands threw the closet doors apart so fast I thought they might have broken. As soon as I saw her clothes were still there, I sagged against the wall in relief. She was still here.

Maybe she was on the back side of the porch? With haste I checked, and she wasn't there. Panic started settling in again, that something had happened to her, but then I saw a lone figure out in the moonlit water.

My goddess of the sea.

Not even thinking twice, I ripped my shirt over my head and took my shoes off.

My feet carried me to her like we were magnets feeling the pull. The water was warm as it crashed against me, my eyes never leaving the girl sitting on a board facing the full moon.

I swam over to her, and even though I could still touch the bottom, I needed to get to her now.

She must have heard me coming because she turned the board around to watch me approach.

Silhouetted by the moon, she looked like an angel. She was so beautiful. I didn't feel like I deserved her.

My hand touched the board to help me tread water, and I tried to find the words to explain myself. They just wouldn't come. Her black hair was down, and her tanned skin shimmered in the light.

"I'm sorry. I promise I will never walk away like that again. I've never done this, and I wasn't thinking about anything other than just us being together. Including the repercussions. I swear to you, Alessandra, I will do whatever it takes for us to be together. I see my future in your eyes; I always have."

There was nothing but the silence of the night between us, and I was hoping that she was going to dive right in with me, following my lead.

"Talk to me."

"Please," I begged, needing to hear her thoughts. She could end this right now, and I had to hear it from her lips if that was what she wanted.

"'Can't Help Falling in Love,' Elvis Presley." Her voice was low but clear as could be to my ears.

She was falling in love with me.

Without letting another second pass, I lifted myself up onto her board. She wasn't prepared for my intentions but held on and helped balance us as I situated myself. My hands sought the back of her neck and pulled her lips to mine.

"I've already been there; I never stood a chance. Never even thought to fight it."

We let our body do the rest of the talking, there were no other words needed. We lavished each other with passionate kisses. With an amazing amount of balance and core strength, she eased herself on her back and took me with her.

I'd never had sex on a surfboard, but I had a feeling we were about to test it out. At least she had grabbed the long board, which was longer and bigger, and more stable.

My body covered hers, while I held myself up by my elbows. Her legs came out of the water and wrapped themselves around my waist.

We moved together as if we were making love on the board, but there was no way in hell we could truly make it work. Feeling the desire to claim her wrapped around my chest, I rolled us into the water, making sure she stayed above the surface.

"Hold onto the board." My feet touched the sand and my hands gripped her hips, bringing her close to me. Those legs stayed around my waist, where they belonged. She did as I asked, and her arms stretched across the board for balance.

With her body supported by the weightlessness of the water and the board, my fingers drifted to the back of her neck. Untying the little knot, the straps gaveway for her breasts to be exposed in the moonlight.

"Stunning." I leaned down and gave each one a hot kiss, my tongue lingering on her tight budded nipples.

She gasped and wiggled against my cock.

"I know, love, I need you too. So bad." The last two words were strained. With some effort I managed to loosen my trunks, then moved on to her bikini bottom. The little strings on the side made it easy to give us the access we required.

"Say it, Alessandra."

She looked me in the eyes, and with that sexy glint holding me hostage, she gave me the words I wanted.

"I'm yours, Joel. Now please put your D in my P," she said with a smile, and that was all it took.

Chapter Twenty-Five

Alessandra

I was full in a matter of seconds after I gave him what I knew he wanted to hear.

We groaned in unison, both of us overwhelmed by the sensation of him filling me to the hilt.

"Oh, God, Joel. Move." It was a matter of life or death.

"Whatever my girl wants. Jesus Christ, you're gripping the shit out of me." He breathed in and out, and pulled out then pumped back in. Yes! I knew we wouldn't have much more time in the water when it came to lubrication, even though I was soaked, the ocean would wash away all evidence of that. But he was getting me there, God was he getting me there.

His fingers dug into my ass as he lifted me up and slammed me down on his cock. All I could do was grip the board for dear life.

"So perfect," he groaned, and then his lips sought out mine. Without thinking, I abandoned the board and wrapped my arms around his shoulders, my nails digging in deep.

He hissed from the pain, but it only made him fuck me harder, hitting just the spot I needed.

"Oh, please keep going, right there. Ah! Oh!" I was about to lose it. The water was just as restless around us as he nailed into me.

His teeth nipped at my opened lips.

"Come for me," he growled and moved his head from my lips to my neck, burying himself in there, kissing me, biting the sensitive skin.

"Oh, fuck!" I groaned. My eyes found the moon above me, and I felt like I was there, floating with stars.

Joel pushed harder and chased down his own release. His groan of pure ecstasy made me shudder, feeling like another orgasm was on the horizon.

"Alessandra," he moaned, and I grabbed his head, pulling his lips back to mine, needing to breath in his moans, filling my lungs with his pleasure.

He stood there, holding me in his arms, my board pulling against the tether to my ankle. His silence began to concern me.

"You okay?"

"Never letting you go, Lips."

I curled my body into his, feeling safe, and knew he would treat me with care in every way I needed him to.

Despite the change in weight, he walked us out of the water, his cock still inside me. I reached down to untie the Velcro tether from the board, leaving the board in the sand. I'd make Joel replace it, if it went back out to sea.

We had more important things to take care of.

"Bed?" I panted as he walked up the porch, his still-hard cock hitting me deep with each step.

"Nope. The hammock." He sat down and lay back, with me straddled on top of him. Time for round two. We quickly got rid of our wet clothing and became a tangled, naked mess.

"You really can't go again, can you?" I asked, feeling a little amazed that his dick hadn't truly softened.

"Told you there wasn't anything I couldn't do." He smirked, looking every bit the cocky asshole that made me fall for him.

Slowly I dragged myself up his cock and slammed back down, riding him, with the sway of the hammock helping me.

His hands moved up and down my back, feeling my skin, driving my senses wild.

My legs were burning from the workout, but it was so worth it. His mouth reached up and grabbed hold of my nipple, sucking and teasing. My head fell back with a hearty moan.

I can't believe I wasted time fighting this.

The more he gripped me with his hands and mouth, the closer I got. My pace quickened, and I started to wiggle back and forth, over and over. Every movement rubbed my clit, and pressed his dick right where I needed it.

Oh, cheese and crackers.

"Oh, God, I'm gonna come."

Feeling like I needed the help, his hands went to my hips and moved me back and forth over him with extra pressure. Which I'll be honest, and admit the orgasm that was coming my way was making me lose momentum, so his efforts were appreciated. It felt too good to keep going.

"Keep riding my dick, Alessandra, fuck.I'm close. Look at me." My head snapped back and my eyes met his, blue meeting blue.

"So fucking beautiful." I felt him expand inside me and then he let it all go, throwing me into orgasmic bliss along with him.

I woke up the next morning feeling both gloriously sated and disgusting.

Joel was trying to sneak out of the hammock we both fell asleep in, without waking me. Not sneaky enough this time, movie star.

"I feel sticky. Like all over." I was covered in ocean salt, sand, sweat, and Joel's love juice. Yeah, I was in need of a serious shower. Stat.

"Shower before breakfast?" He held his hand out to help me up, and I took it. He pulled a little extra hard, pulling me right into his body. It felt like a car hitting a wall.

I was about to let him have it when he kissed me, then walked us to the large stone-tiled bathroom.

Honest to God, I think I moaned when the salty tangles in my hair started to smooth out enough that I could run my fingers through it. The water was heavenly, and I was so happy to be clean again.

"So." I looked at Joel, and pumped some of his shampoo in my hand. He leaned down so I could run my fingers through his hair, paying extra attention to that little gray patch in the front.

"Let's just take one step at a time."

"Okay." I would try. Joel was what I wanted, so I would make it work.

"So tell me, Lips. Where did you get this scar?" He pointed to a mark on the side of my right breast.

This was embarrassing.

"Um, back when I was thirteen, I tried to beat the boys in my neighborhood at everything. Including jumping my bike over a ramp." The memory came to me, clear as day. Me in my ripped jeans and *Born to be Bad* T-shirt, on my bike. I pedaled so fast, and thought I was going to make it.

"I failed epically. My tire just went over the ramp straight down to the ground. I flew face-first towards the dirt, but the handlebar rammed right into my breast and scraped off the skin." I didn't cry, though. Nope, I walked myself back to my house with my bike and then screamed when my mom poured hydrogen peroxide on it. I couldn't wear a bra for a whole month. It was unbearable to have anything touching the wound besides a shirt.

"I can see it. Badass Alessandra, even at thirteen." He smiled, and I pushed his head back into the spray to wash the shampoo out of his hair.

Chapter Twenty-Six

Alessandra

Today's shoot was a fun one. I got to watch Joel pretend to drown in four feet of water, then face-plant into the sand before crawling to the shade of a palm tree. I got to add some fun prosthetics to his face to make it look like he had a busted eyebrow and a cut on his cheek.

Kandi waggled her eyes at me once then popped her bubble and focused on the acting before us.

When lunchtime came around, Joel was so hungry he didn't even try to clean up before heading for the table of fresh fruits and sandwiches that had been set out under a pop-up tent.

"So good," he moaned and devoured one sandwich, with his eyes set on another.

We were back in our normal flow of things, so why change habits now that we were sleeping together?

I grabbed a carrot and saw the sandwich in his hand stalled on its way to his mouth. I acted like I was going to put on another bite show for him, but instead just ate the carrot normally.

"Can't fool me now; I know the truth." He winked and walked over to his chair so I could touch up his fake blood.

We worked like nothing was different, and when the day was over, we waited till everyone cleared out before heading back to the house.

I needed to call Jenson to check on him, so as soon as we walked through the door I sat on the couch and pressed dial on his name.

He was having fun, which made me happy, and helped me feel better about being away from him. I missed him so much.

He launched into stories about what he and my parents had done since I left, and I told him about the house we were in, and today's shoot. He yawned, and I told him to go ahead and get some rest. It was time for bed in Brazil.

Once we were off the phone, I sat there feeling a little homesick for Jenson.

"Wanting anything particular for dinner?" Joel asked from the kitchen.

"Comfort food." I was in the mood to just hang out and stuff my face with something to make me feel better about my boy being so far away. It was still another three and a half weeks before I'd see him again in person. I'd be okay. I knew that. But I still missed him.

"All right." He shut the fridge door and pulled out his phone to order us some pizza. I thought that was a good choice.

"Wanna talk about it?" He came and sat next to me, pulling me in to rest on his chest. It was a nice place to snuggle so I went easily.

"I just miss him. We've done this once before and he has a blast. It's good for him to get to spend time with my family; I just hate being away from him for so long."

"Anything I can do?" He gave me a little hug and then started rubbing my back.

"Nope, I'll get over it in a little bit. Wanna watch a movie?"

He smiled and grabbed the remote. Joel was obviously not just an actor but a movie fan as well. Movies truly were his passion, every part of them. Not that I would ever ask it of him anyway, but he would never be absolutely happy without the movie life.

Last night we just both accepted that we were in love, and everything was just going to have to work out. Whether we stay secret, or let it all out of the bag, we wanted each other. Jenson was all for it, too, so I was thankful I didn't have to deal with a child who hated the person I wanted. I would always choose my son.

The pizza man showed up thirty minutes later, and we just chilled together, ate, and watched two movies. When it was time to settle in for the night, we climbed into bed and made out. No sex, just kissing. It was sweet, and I liked that. Sometimes love was this all-consuming power that drove people to forget who they are. We were us, Joel and Alessandra.

He fell asleep first, and I just looked at him, memorizing every hair on his jaw, the straightness of his nose, the lips that were a darker pink from kissing me so much. His eyelashes were so long that I was slightly jealous. And that cute little gray patch. Something about it just drove me wild. He was right around thirty years old and just embraced it. I wish I could say the same. I was probably going to start coloring my hair as soon as the first gray hair showed up. Thankfully, it hadn't happened yet, but with Jenson still heading into his teenage years, I knew I would end up with a bunch by the time he graduated.

Sleep finally took me over peacefully. I dreamed of paradise, swimming with fish, Jenson telling me there was a shark feeding frenzy going on, and Joel in the kitchen wearing nothing but an apron.

"You're dreaming of me. How cute."

"Nope, dreaming of Thor, and his mighty hammer." I snuggled into his bare chest, knowing I wasn't going to be staying there much longer. He would retaliate in some way for my comment.

He rolled himself on top of me, his very own hard hammer lying on my belly.

"Wench, thou shall not think of any man's hammer but mine." He pretended to talk like Thor, and it was cute.

I opened my eyes and peered at the clock beside the bed.

"We don't have any time. Gotta get dressed and over to set." I was disappointed that I wouldn't get a morning orgasm to start the day.

"We got this." He smiled, then proceeded to prove me wrong on the time subject. We were sated, clothed, fed, and in the Jeep in twenty minutes. He was good. There was no denying that once he put his mind to something, Joel was unstoppable.

Chapter Twenty-Seven

Joel

Our first week in Kauai was gone in a flash, and the second was close to being over too. Alessandra and I were in paradise, together. We worked, we came back to the house or explored, then we either cuddled up for the night or had fantastic sex. I liked how things with her were so easy. No fumbling around trying to figure out what you can and can't do around them. We just fit together in a way I couldn't have imagined.

Filming was almost over, and I was excited as hell to see the finished product. The work wasn't over for me. I would have to go back and do voiceovers, then start the promoting process. TV shows, guest appearances, interviews. Those few months before release day were going to be crazy.

But I knew she'd be there. I'd have them both, Jenson and Alessandra, by my side, or waiting for me at home.

Alessandra was out in the sand, soaking up the sun, while I was handling some things on my laptop. I had investments, endorsement deals, and charities I still had to take care of.

She came bouncing back inside the house a few minutes later in just her bikini, looking sexy as hell. I'd come to know every curve, every scar, every part of her she thought was maybe a flaw but I found sexy. Her C-section scar? I licked it every chance I got. She had a baby cut out of her, and then had to take care of the kid while healing. If that wasn't badass, I didn't know what was.

That scar on her breast? I kissed the shit out of it every time. Where she thought she had thicker thighs than some? Oh yeah, I paid attention to them.

There was not one piece of her that I didn't find attractive and want to worship.

She grabbed a drink from the fridge and sat next to me.

"Looking extra tan there, Lips." She had really blossomed here, looking every bit the Brazilian she was. Mouth-watering.

"Whatcha doing?" She ignored my first comment.

"Scheduling a children's visit dressed up as Stryder." My comic book character. Another actor, who played in the film, and I liked to do this once a month, dress up and go to a children's hospital and play it up. The kids loved it, and we felt like bringing a smile to their face would help them. Even just for a day, they could laugh and forget about the cards they had been dealt.

"You big mush bunny." She grinned, and I knew she liked it. I was a big old softy at heart.

"You weren't saying I was a big softy last night. Actually, I remember you saying how my cock was so hard that—" She smacked my arm before I could finish my sentence.

"Yeah, yeah, shut your face."

I just smiled and went back to work.

Then an email popped up from my publicist.

I heard a gasp from beside me, and knew Alessandra was reading it along with me.

We were outed. Paps caught us hanging out on set together and then hiking in the mountains yesterday. There were pictures of her applying makeup to my face, and then there was the one with packs on our backs, kissing by a waterfall. The shot was pretty clear, so there was no denying it.

My publicist wanted to know what the deal was, and letting me know the best way to handle the situation in a positive light for me.

Instead of reading over his lists of suggestions, I turned to Alessandra, needing to know how she felt right now. This was her fear, and it was happening.

She wasn't smiling, which worried me.

"It's okay," she said, looking at me and nodding her head.

"We knew it was going to happen at some point. I know Lisa won't fire me with only one and a half weeks left. We can do this." She was obviously very shaken, but she was putting on a brave face for me.

"We can. It's going to be fine." I placed the laptop on the coffee table and pulled her into my lap. She was not doing okay, regardless of what she said.

"Hey, I love you. Remember? They can't touch us." I looked her in the eyes and reminded her how serious we were. We could do it. We were both strong enough.

"Right." She was nervous, and I needed to find a way to ease her thoughts right now.

"Come on, let's go take a bath." I lifted her up and walked her out to the hammock. She sat there while I got the outside bathtub ready. I had bubbles and bath bombs ready to go. I wasn't much of a lotion man, so I took baths to ease my sore muscles and the bath bombs helped moisturize my skin. I much preferred it to lathering up every morning and evening like most people did. Two baths a week and I had sexy, smooth skin.

When the bath was done, I helped her get out of her bikini—because I was a gentleman like that—then stripped down and joined her in the tub.

I sat in the back, and she nestled herself against my chest. The bubbles surrounded us, and I could feel her body start to relax a little, but she was still tense.

Using my thumbs, I started massaging the tops of her shoulders, hoping that would take her mind off the email.

"I'll be all right, Joel. It's just going to take some getting used to. I'm not going anywhere." She tilted her head up to look at me, and I kissed her nose.

I believed her, but I still wanted to ease her mind at the moment.

A grin appeared on my face when an idea struck my head. I didn't know if it would work, but it couldn't hurt trying.

"Ever used one of these?" I reached over and grabbed a bath bomb. It was a large, pink one that fizzed, made up of all natural ingredients.

"Yeah, but my bath is half this size, so it isn't as nice to use." She was thinking about something else, so that was a start.

I set it in the tub, right between her legs. I knew the fizzing had reached her sensitive sex when she jumped in my arms.

"What are you doing?"

"Just feel it, and feel me." My hand grazed her body and joined the bubbles on her clit.

She gasped, and I knew this was working out the way it did in my head. The bubbles would have an almost vibrator effect on her while I helped pull the orgasm out of her.

"Oh boy." She took a deep breath and let it happen. Once the bath bomb was done, I grabbed another, this one more powerful, and she let out a little whimper when I placed it closer, and pressed two fingers inside her.

She was getting close, the combination of my fingers and the bubbles was working her over good. Giving her the extra push, I kissed her sweet neck and my other hand went to kneading her breasts. My cock was hard, and I wanted nothing more than to sink into her heat when she came.

"Sit up," I commanded, and she listened.

"Grip the edge of the tub in front of you," I growled, needing to be inside her now. She did as I said, and I adjusted myself so I was on my knees behind her. I grabbed another bath bomb, knowing I was probably overdoing it, and we were going to need a shower after this from how oily we were going to be, but I didn't care.

Placing it in the water beneath her cunt, I aimed my dick and thrust forward. She cried out a slew of curses, and I smacked her ass and pounded her with everything I had.

Her knuckles were turning white, she was gripping the tub so hard. I felt her pussy start to quiver and knew she was about to explode. Both my hands gripped onto her hip bones, and I pushed harder.

She detonated, pulling me with her.

My fingers dug in, and there were going to be some marks on her hips, but I would kiss the shit out of them every time I saw them, too.

Every orgasm with her felt better than the first. When she finally came down, I had to catch her body so she wouldn't fall into the water face first.

I held her in my arms, knowing I gave her peace of mind, even if for a little bit.

Chapter Twenty-Eight

Alessandra

Well, I was never going to be able to look at bath bombs the same ever again.

Joel and I needed a shower after our bath, so we went straight from the tub to the bathroom and cleaned off all that bomb oil.

I was still a little nervous about how things were going to be at work in the morning, but I was in love with Joel, and he was in love with me. So beyond that, I wouldn't care what others thought.

That was easier said than done.

That morning, I had some women that had never talked to me on set, asking about Joel in bed. Others kept giving me glares of jealousy. And I even saw some guys trying to give Joel a high-five for nailing his makeup artist.

I held my head up high, but I could see the tension in Joel's eyes as some of the idiot men gave me the once-over.
He was going to end up fighting someone if I didn't do

something. When Leighton called a break and pulled him aside to talk to him, I knew it wasn't just me seeing his anger starting to rise. It was affecting his job.

He walked over to his chair, and I wrapped my arms around him to give him comfort.

"'The Man,' by Aloe Blacc."

He huffed, but I saw his face soften slightly at my attempt to calm him.

"I'm fine, Joel. Ignore them; they aren't in a relationship with you. I am." I grabbed his jaw and made him look me in the eye. It was just us right now.

He went back to the set, and everything was calmed down for now. We were presenting a solid front, and I had faith it wouldn't get worse.

When our final week of shooting began, I was tired, but Joel and I had managed not to kill anyone. So I considered it a success.

A knock on the door in the morning woke me up, and Joel, who was already making us breakfast, went to open it.

"Right on time, bud."

Not caring that I was wearing just my underwear and one of Joel's shirts, I leaped out of the bed at the sound of Jenson's voice.

He was standing there giving Joel a fist bump, and I almost tackled him to the ground. I missed him so much, and now he was here!

"Oh my God, how are you here? I'm so happy!" I couldn't stop talking, hugging him, and kissing his face.

"Okay, Mom. Geez." He pushed me off and tried to compose himself. He was a teenager, and teenagers didn't hug their moms for that long.

"I brought him," Joel piped up, looking very proud of himself.

"Yeah, I'm here for the week, then head back with you." Jenson dropped his bag, and looked around, totally ignoring me, who was practically crying I was so happy to see him.

"Jenson Cole Rose, you get your butt back here and give your mom a hug and tell me you missed me." I wasn't having anything less. He rolled his eyes, but came over and did as he was told, with a little extra squeeze in his hug. He missed me, too.

We didn't have too much time to sit down for breakfast, but it was still nice having Jenson here with me. He was excited to be on set with me as my assistant. He wore swim trunks and a normal black T-shirt. Sort of imitating Joel, but I didn't say anything to him.

The rest of the day went pretty easily. Although we had gotten used to the people on set talking about us dating behind our backs, Jenson had noticed, and he wasn't very happy about it.

"Want me to punch them?" He clenched his fists while looking at the men that were trying to goad me with lewd gestures. They all thought I was easy, since Joel had gotten me in the sack. Joel had barely held himself back the week before, and I sort of felt sorry for these guys once filming was over and Joel could let loose. Technically even then he shouldn't go after them, but there was only so much he could take while keeping his mouth shut. They were pressing their luck. I pulled my kid in close and gave him a little hug.

"Maybe an accidental nut shot." He smiled, and I didn't really care if he took my joke seriously or not.

We both watched as Joel and Nineveh embraced each other tenderly and kissed. It was their final scene together, when she finally confessed her love to him, and he escaped the book that held him hostage.

"You really like him?" Jenson asked, while watching the two actors. I still didn't like it that his lips were touching another's right now, but it wasn't real. He wasn't kissing her like he kissed me, and he wasn't holding her like he held me.

"Yeah, I do."

Joel's eyes caught mine briefly when they separated, just to make sure I hadn't ran away.

It wasn't easy, but I was still here. I just prayed I was allowed to work on set if they needed to do any retakes. Lisa had said something to me briefly about being professional, but since we had no incidents during work hours, she didn't make a big deal out of it.

"You good with all the crazy that comes with him?" I needed to know that Jenson had an understanding about fame, and what it does to your life.

He nodded slowly, and I hoped he really got it. This was probably going to be one wild ride.

Chapter Twenty-Nine

Joel

"Please? I swear, we'll be quick," I whispered, as my hands gripped Alessandra's ass while she leaned against the couch. Jenson was watching a movie with us, and I needed some alone time with my woman.

It had been a few days, and we only had one day left before filming was over, and we flew home.

Life with a teenager was not as easy. I couldn't have sex with Alessandra on the table, or in the outside tub. We had to wait until he was asleep, or sneak off into the bathroom, so he wouldn't hear us.

He wasn't a dirty kid, so that was a plus. But I had noticed a Tumblr notification pop up on his phone for something dirty. Alessandra didn't know that Tumblr was pretty much for porn nowadays, so I had to be the one to break it to her that his collection was all digital. She had a rough night that night, trying to accept he was growing up.

"I can hear you two," Jenson muttered, and I gave her ass one last squeeze before going back to just sitting next to her like an adult.

Alessandra's phone starting ringing, and she answered it with a very feminine hello, then yanked the phone away from her ear because very high-pitched screaming was coming from the speaker.

"Oh my God, put us on speaker, so Joel can hear this!" It was Livia's voice, and she was very excited. I smiled, having a feeling where this conversation was going to go. I was very good at reading my friend.

"Okay, you're on." Alessandra had put her on speaker and held the phone out so it wasn't too close to our eardrums.

"Killian and I are getting married!"

Alessandra squealed her excitement along with Livia, who couldn't stop talking about it in a very high-pitchedrush of words.

I was right; Killian wouldn't waste much time without making her his in every way he could. I grabbed my phone and sent him a text, congratulating him.

Since I had been filming, and he had Livia on the road with him, we hadn't talked much. Which was good, in a way. We were still friends and would see each other, but I wasn't his only friend anymore. He had her to shine light on his life and keep him happy.

Livia kept Alessandra on the phone for over an hour, talking about wedding stuff. Of course, those two had become friends, talking on the phone, and on Facebook. Livia had gotten her to read some romance novels, and I tried to get her to put that knowledge to good use, but it didn't work out so well for me. Because of course she put on the front that she wanted to strap me down and shove dildos up my ass. That was not a joke I found funny.

I was still a little traumatized from that conversation, and it happened last week.

Jenson's phone dinged, and he looked at it, then put it down. His face hardened a little.

"Sup, kid?"

"Nothin'." He was short with me and abruptly stood and walked into the room he was sleeping in. Odd. Alessandra hadn't noticed what just happened, so I figured I would let her have her time with Livia and go talk to him myself, hoping I wasn't overstepping somehow.

I knocked on his door before entering, and he was sitting there, his hair a mess from running his hands through it.

"Wanna talk?" I closed the door behind me, in case he didn't want his mom hearing it.

"Just stupid kids from school." He wasn't too thrilled to be talking about it, but I could tell he needed to, so I just stayed quiet and listened.

"The stuff they are saying about us in those magazines. I don't care, but I don't wanna hear it coming from people at school, ya know?"

"I do." I didn't want my fame screwing with his school life.

"But I don't want you and Mom to break up. You're a cool guy, and I've never seen Mom like this. She's never dated anyone since I can remember, so it's a big deal." That was good to hear. He was still on my side when it came to his mom. I didn't want to break up with her, either.

"I'll get over it. They're just being stupid." He cracked his knuckles and lay back against the bed.

"My dad always used to say, if you can't change your friends, then change your friends. So the ones that are talking shit aren't your friends. The true ones wouldn't disrespect you like that. You are smarter than they are." I hoped I helped him a little; I didn't really know how to be a philosophical parental figure, but I could give him honesty.

"You need anything, just let me know." He needed time, and I knew the feeling. He just nodded and went back to focusing on the dark ocean through the window.

I found Alessandra sitting on the couch, saying goodbye to Livia.

"She seems excited."

Cue rolling of the eyes.

"She's marrying the love of her life. Of course, she's excited. Sounds like they are going to have a laid-back wedding at his house in the Keys. Sounds like fun." She sounded tired, and I'm sure she was. Between everything going on with work, Jenson, and all our extra activities, she needed rest.

I sat next to her and hauled her legs on top of mine. My hands found her feet, rubbing them, hoping to release any tension in her body.

"We should get married in Hawaii," I suggested. Half being serious, half not. When I asked her to marry me, it wasn't going to be like that. Boring. It just wasn't our style.

We were like Deadpool and Vanessa.

Minus the International Women's Day celebrating part.

"I'm thinking more like Alaska. A fur panty and bra set can be pretty sexy for a wedding night outfit." Somehow, she couldn't ruin the image of her on our future wedding night with fur lingerie. Nope.

We were quiet for a little while, me massaging her feet as she just enjoyed the moment.

"Where'd Jenson go?" Her eyes closed, and her head dropped back to the pillow behind her.

"He went out to go knock up a Hawaiian girl named Lola."

Her lips lifted up and she spoke.

"Are they drinking champagne that tastes like Coca-Cola?"

How could anyone deny that this woman and I were meant to be? Truly, she was like the girl version of me. Music, surfing, movies, and fun humor. She couldn't cook for shit, but I was fine with handling that. I swear, I could never get over how perfect she was for me.

"I think I'm ready for bed." She yawned, and my hands slid up her legs, feeling her soft skin.
I reached around her back and picked her up like the superhero I was.

She didn't fight me as I carried her to the bedroom, and we settled into bed together. She passed out quickly, and I just lay there, holding her in my arms.

Two more days in paradise, then it was back to our true reality. I wasn't ready for us to go back to Los Angeles. Here we really only had to deal with people on set, there we would be dealing with everyone. Women who thought they were going to be the ones to make me settle. Shitty guys I would have to beat for thinking that she would sleep around since she slept with me.

I just wish I'd thought of the shit hitting the fan before we reached the mainland.

Maybe I could have been better prepared.

Chapter Thirty

Alessandra

"Cheers!"

Everyone lifted their champagne glasses in celebration of the final day of filming. It was a crazy four months, and I was happy to have a little break before my next job. I was in such a good mood, I pretended not to notice Jenson taking a sip of champagne. I also had to smother a grin when he made a disgusted face and didn't drink the rest.

Joel was surrounded by a bunch of people, all talking about how great he did with the role. He really did do a fantastic job. I was sure it was going to be his best yet.

"You did a good job during the film. You've got real skill." Nineveh had made her way close to me and smiled politely. We hadn't really talked much since she came onto the set, not even a hello.

"Thanks. You did wonderfully, too. It's going to be a big hit." Besides kissing Joel for her job, she hadn't done anything to me to warrant bitchy behavior. Her hair was wrapped up in a bun, and her dress was blowing in the beach breeze.

"Thanks. It's the biggest film I've done." She blushed, and I had a feeling this girl was very shy.

There was an awkward silence between us, and before I could break it up, she beat me to it.

"I'm sorry if our job caused you two any stress. He's very much in love with you. I knew that even before you guys were outed." She offered me a smile, and seemed very genuine.

"Thanks. It was hard, but I know we are real."

"It's beautiful. I hope I find love like that one day." She was cute, but quiet. Very much opposite of me.

"Well, I don't wanna take up any more of your time. Maybe I'll see you on another set sometime." She wrinkled her nose in an adorable bunny way, then floated off, her dress billowing behind her.

I liked her, and judging from the way Leighton eyed her, he did too. Interesting. Maybe love wasn't too far off for her.

Just as I went to grab a piece of cake, my phone started ringing. I ignored it, because it couldn't be more important than cake right now.

When it rang again almost immediately, I sighed and pressed the button to answer. Realizing too late who I had just accepted a call from.

"What do you want?"

"Sweet as pie. You never change." The gruff male voice over the phone boiled my blood.

"What do you want, Alex?" *You stupid, son of a bitch ex-boyfriend of mine.*

I wish I would have said that out loud to him, but I didn't want to cause a scene. So I walked away from the celebrating crowd and hid behind a dune so I could yell at him if I needed to.

"Just wanted to call you on your shit. Been waiting a long time for this moment."

Is he fucking kidding me right now?

"I swear, Alex, get it out. You calling to give me some excuse again why you never wanted to see our son? How big your next movie is going to be? I don't care. We've lived without you perfectly." He did call sometimes to brag about his life, which wasn't anything spectacular. Landed a commercial for Viagra? Well, you were the perfect candidate, since you have issues there.

"I was just sitting her scrolling on my phone, when I see your name pop up everywhere on the news. Dating Joel Kline, huh? He really must be a better actor than me, to get you to stay around with him, living the Hollywood life."

Despite feeling strong when it came to him, what he said had dug a little hole in my thoughts.

"You can't believe those stupid things, and really, Alex? Unless you want me to take you to court again, and this time bring up how you've never paid child support, I suggest you leave me alone."

"You didn't wanna live that life with me, and I'm the father to our kid." I scoffed at that. He was never a father to Jenson.

"It's different." Why I felt the need to justify myself to him, I had no clue.

"Sure it is. He's just more convincing than me. So I'm just going to enjoy this moment, and watch for the fall. Because we both know the curtain will close at some point."

"Oh, go fuck another whore, Alex." I ended the call, but he had already done his job of riling me up. Why do I always answer when he calls? I think some small part of me hopes that he is calling to apologize, or see the error of his ways and try to make amends with his son. Maybe be a dad, for once. But it never was for that. Always something stupid, and I couldn't care less.

Whatever. I wasn't going to let what he said bother me. Joel was real with me.

I went back to the party and tried to enjoy myself, but it was like Alex just poured vinegar in my tea. I couldn't shake it.

Joel came over to check on me and then stayed close while we talked to people. Jenson was chatting a mile a minute with one of the cameramen, who told him he'd done a lot of underwater shooting.

"You okay?" Joel leaned over and asked in my ear, and I nodded with a fake smile. His eyes narrowed in response, and he knew something was wrong. I just didn't want to talk about it.

When the celebration started to die out, we drove back to the house, and I tried to dig myself out of my quicksand thoughts.

"I love you." I wrapped my arms around Joel once we set our stuff down by the door. Jenson went directly to the kitchen and started eating again.

"I love you, too," he said, with no hesitation.

"Ready to tell me what happened?"

I looked into his eyes, and I knew it was wrong, but I couldn't say it. Would he be mad that Alex's words had gotten to me? The scared-of-getting-hurt Alessandra was rearing her head again in my mind.

"I'm just stressing over nothing. I'll get over it." I gave him a kiss, and left for the bathroom.

I believed Joel, and I believed in us. I wasn't going to let Alex screw my life up again.

Chapter Thirty-One

Joel

It'd been a week since we all left Kauai, and I was losing Alessandra.

I don't know what the main component was in the beginning, but being hounded by paparazzi at the airport curb in L.A. didn't help. Neither had all the gossip news, rumors about her being my side chick, or that Jenson had been getting into the Hollywood scene of drugs and sex that some teens in the business do.

All of it would calm down once our relationship wasn't new anymore. But it was a lot harder than even I was expecting. She was trying, and Jenson too. He didn't care that much, but he did care about his mom. He wanted to protect her, now that he was older. Both of them protecting each other was really all they ever truly had. Her family was in Brazil, and Jenson's dad was a shithead.

I didn't know anything else I could do to help her. This world was hard, and I couldn't be there all the time to watch over them.

I'd stayed the night in her apartment once, and it turned into a disaster.

She and I wound up in the paper indecently dressed. She was in sleep shorts and a tank top, and me in just trunks, with no shirt. I was heading to the beach for a swim, but the wind blew the right way and showed off more of her ass than I would have liked to have been seen by people.

Someone was waiting and caught it at the right moment.

I invited them over to my house in La Jolla for a break, and she thought it was a good idea, to get out of the big city.

Seeing their car pulling into my drive was like taking a breath of fresh air in a stagnant world.

"Hey, guys!" Jenson gave me a nod, but didn't say hello like usual. As he passed me, I couldn't help but notice the bruise under his eye.

"Don't ask," Alessandra huffed, and grabbed her bag, which I took from her and carried into the house.

"Fight?" I couldn't not ask. This was a big deal, if it was. She took a deep breath and went straight for my liquor cabinet.

"Yep. Some kid at the beach that goes to Jenson's school made some comment, and Jenson punched him. Thank God it didn't happen at school; he would have probably been suspended. This was just on the beach, so they were pulled apart, and he came home." She grabbed the tequila and took a long sip. Shit. That wasn't good.

"I'm sorry," I muttered, feeling like hell that this was happening because of her relationship with me.

"I know. It'll blow over one day. Jenson is still good with us, that is all that matters to me." I heard her words, but it didn't stop that nagging feeling.

After she got buzzed, and her worries disappeared for a night, she was smiling and laughing again. I missed her. This Alessandra had been buried beneath the stressed mother that had a life to protect. Jenson was acting normal again, too. We surfed, and had dinner together. I talked about how I was going to appear in a few panels at the big Comic-Con convention at the end of this month, and told him that I would get him and Alessandra some passes. He was nothing but grins after that.

When Alessandra crashed in my bed from the alcohol, I sat there looking at her with a heavy heart.

Maybe I was being selfish, wanting a life with them, all while dragging their family through the mud.

I knew it was going to blow over, but at what cost will it take to get there?

Jenson getting in more fights? He was thirteen, hormones and everything else going on was hard enough.

Her job? I hoped it didn't have any effect on that. Lisa liked her, and said she would always recommend her. She didn't have a contract with a particular studio. I'd hoped with this past movie under her belt that she would land a studio gig, but she hadn't heard anything yet. Leighton said he'd talk to them about it, since he agreed she did a good job.

I felt like I was destroying them.

Feeling the need to breathe some air, I left her sleeping peacefully in my bed, and walked outside. I dialed the only person I knew would answer at this hour.

"Hey," Killian answered, on the third ring.

"This shit sucks."

"Care to be more specific?"

"I'm destroying their lives." I heard him huff at my statement.

"A little dramatic."

"They can't go anywhere without trouble. Jenson got in a fight over gossip about him and his mom. Alessandra headed straight for the tequila bottle when she got here." My head fell in my hands as I sat on the chair by the unlit fire pit.

"You've been through it before; this time you just care more."

Well, he was right about that. I had cared about past girlfriends, but not this way. I would have never contemplated letting them go so they could be happier without me.

"I'm thinking of ending it, so they don't have to deal with it anymore." As soon as the words came out, I hated it. I didn't want to do that.

"We both know I'm not the best at this shit. I gave Livia space and time. I took her to the airport myself. But in the end, we were all that mattered. The space was needed on her end, and when she came back it was like the time apart never happened."

I was with him after he let her go. He fell to shit, but still managed to live as best as he could, which wasn't much. She had her space to figure out her life and then she came back to him. Now they were getting married.

"I don't know what to do."

"Wish I had the answer. You've always been there for me. If I can help, I'll try."

There was silence between us, because there was no advice to be given on his end, and I didn't have any answers. He was just being there for me, if I needed it.

"I'm gonna talk to her."

"Good plan."

It was the only plan I had. Alessandra and I needed to talk it out like adults.

Killian and I hung up the phone, and I went to the water and stuck my toes in the waves, thinking about what I was going to say to my sleeping beauty when she woke up.

I didn't go to sleep that night. Instead I walked the beach. When the sun barely started to light up the sky I decided to continue walking to the little convenience store to pick up some fresh bananas for my signature banana pancakes.

Alessandra and Jenson both loved them, and I was happy to make them breakfast.

While I was looking over the bunches of bananas, a woman approached me.

"Hey, you're Joel Kline, right?" I smiled, giving her the official Joel Kline smile.

"Yep. How are you doing?" I held my hand out, and she shook it.

"I'm doing great. I'm sorry to bother you at the store, but I don't think I'll get another chance to do this." She was blonde, pretty toned, with green eyes, and most likely in her late thirties. She was wearing scrubs.

"What can I do for you?" I was polite.

"I work at All Children's Hospital."

She went on to tell me about this big fundraiser they were doing and trying to raise money to help families who needed a little extra assistance when paying for medical bills and lodging. The whole fundraiser was going to be a carnival, and some of the kids could go and participate, but some wouldn't be able to leave their rooms. She wanted to know if I would be interested in dressing up and entertaining the kids that couldn't be around crowds or go outside. I asked for her card and told her I'd call, then walked her to her car. It sounded like an exhausting day, but totally worth it.

By the time I made it back to the house, Alessandra and Jenson were up already.

Chapter Thirty-Two

Alessandra

"Hello, honey, I'm home!" Joel's voice echoed through the house to the kitchen table where I was having coffee, and Joel was eating some yogurt he found in the fridge.

I wasn't sure if he had even come to bed last night; he wasn't there when I woke up in the middle of the night to pee, and he wasn't there when I woke up this morning. I was used to not waking up with him, but he was usually making breakfast or working out.

"I got bananas for pancakes." He set them down on the counter and leaned down to kiss me, earning a snicker from Jenson at Joel's display.

"Awesome!" I exclaimed once he pulled back.

He got to work on them, and I enjoyed my coffee while watching him cook. It was the little things.

Yesterday was not a good day for my sanity. Everything was getting to me, and I needed to drink it out.

Which I did. Not that I was wasted, but I was buzzed enough not to care for a few hours.

This morning I was a little better.

We ate our breakfast and then Joel had to disappear into his office to make some phone calls. I went upstairs to get dressed for the day. Maybe we could go for a drive or something fun.

I got dressed and then decided to check and see what else was being spread about us on the internet. I wanted to be prepared if anyone said anything to Jenson. Hopefully I could diffuse the situation before it started.

Then I saw all these pictures of Joel hugging a blonde, by a car that wasn't his. It was from this morning. Early this morning.

I tried to remain calm, there had to be more to this story, but I could feel a little red haze start to cloud my thoughts.

"Give him a chance to explain." I told myself, really trying not to lose my shit right now. I marched into his office just as he was hanging up the phone.

"Lips." He held out his hands for me to come sit in his lap. I did and waited for him to tell me about the blonde.

"I wanted to talk to you about something." His face looked stressed. My stomach started twisting in knots. I stayed quiet and waited for him to explain.

"I'm worried about you and Jenson, with all this shit going on. I know it'll all blow away soon, but I wanted to see if you needed anything from me. Maybe we need to lay low for a little while, until things calm down."

Are you fucking kidding me? I jumped up from his lap and my head popped.

A small part of me knew I was about to overreact, but I was past the point of no return. My blood was on fire, and with all the stress, and Alex's words still ringing in my head, I felt nothing but rage.

"You're breaking up with me?" The look on his face was one of surprise.

"No, I was thinking maybe we should just lay low, and everyone would leave us alone." He stood up and tried to approach me.

"No, I get it. Loud and clear. When were you going to tell me about your little tromp this morning, huh?" His head tilted to the side at my question.

"I've been beating myself up over how shitty things have been for you and Jenson, so I took a walk and went to the store. Jesus, Alessandra, put the loco back in the box."

And I lost it, grabbing the closest thing to me and throwing it at him. He wanted loco? He was going to get it. Full Brazilian bitch, coming his way.

"What about the fucking blonde that is all over the internet with you? When you should have been in bed with me, you were out with someone else!" I screamed and threw something else. God, Alex was right, how fucking blind was I? I thought we could do it, could handle the madness because we loved each other. But it was all just an act.

"Fuck me." He ran his fingers down his face, and I took that as an admission. Turning around as quickly as I could, I yelled for Jenson to get his shit and meet me at the car. He knew my tone and did as asked, quickly.

"Seriously, Alessandra, whatever you saw is not what you think." He chased me and then grabbed my arm.

"Don't fucking touch me. God, I knew it. I should have never trusted an actor again." I grabbed anything of mine that wasn't in my bag and shoved it in, heading down the stairs with Joel on my heels. He didn't let me get close to the door before gripping me and pushing my body back against the wall.

"You think I've been acting with you this whole time? I could have had your mouth on my dick back in the trailer when you threw yourself at me a while ago. We are real, and that shit you think you know is not what it is. Just calm your tits, and let me explain.

"'Better Together,' Jack Johnson," he growled and kissed me hard. I pushed him back, not willing to let him seduce me out of this. I was done.

"You want a theme song for how I feel this moment? 'Take a Bow,' Rihanna. Now let me leave. I don't wanna be here right now." The look on his face was like I smacked him. What a fine actor he was.

I opened the door, and Jenson was there waiting for me with the keys in the ignition. He asked if I needed anything, and I told him loud music. So together we listened to loud music, and he would put his hand over mine on the gear shift to comfort me. He didn't ask a single question.

The curtain had fallen over the Alessandra and Joel show, just like Alex said it would. Actors can't be trusted. Joel wanted space apart from me and now he had it. He could be with whoever he wanted, and I had a date with Jack tonight after Jenson went to sleep.

Chapter Thirty-Three

Joel

Jacob and Bella?

Jack and Rose?

Rick and Ilsa?

Joel and Alessandra?

What all do they have in common? Epic-failed couples.

I thought I was doing the right thing, suggesting that we lay low, but with everything that had been churning in her head, then seeing pictures of me and that nurse, it had broken the cuckoo from the clock. She wouldn't even let me explain. Those walls that I fought so hard to knock down just shot back up and created a fortress.

I thought about how horribly wrong everything turned while floating in my pool on a unicorn tube. It was a joke from my sister, but it had a spot for my vodka bottle so in the pool we went.

Did Alessandra ever truly let me in? I thought so. Maybe I was wrong.

I woke up the next morning face down on my couch, feeling like shit both physically and mentally. I grabbed my phone and saw a bunch of texts I didn't remember sending.

We need to talk. -Joel

Alessandra, get your sexy ass back to my house. -Joel

That ass is going to be so fucking pink for this shit. -Joel

Just kidding. -Joel

Maybe. -Joel

Please just let me explain. Call me. -Joel

Ims gonnnn caleeeeeeeee tommmmmm. . . . .. I lerv u. -Joel

Obviously that last one I was too drunk or on my way out of consciousness to really text.

She still hadn't called or texted me back, and it was killing me. She thought I cheated, and hadn't been real with her. My only thought was, whatever screwed with her head our last day in Kauai really messed her up, even if she didn't want to admit it. Alessandra was so strong. I knew she and Jenson could have outlasted the paparazzi crap. Something had to have been stirring the pot and seeing those pictures just confirmed the worst in her head. Her fears got to her.

I rolled off the couch, needing to take a piss, and try to be human for the day.

As soon as I showered and forced myself to eat, I kept thinking of all the times I called her crazy and laughed about the type of woman she was. She'd never really proved it until yesterday, and it didn't lessen my love for her. I still loved her so much I could barely breathe without her.

I had officially spooned the lioness and gotten bit.

One thing that mattered now was how I reacted. She didn't want anything to do with me in her head. So where did that leave me?

In the same place I was before our date. Annoying the shit out of her until those walls broke, and she falls in love with me again. I'd wait forever. I really didn't care as long as the outcome was her back in my arms.

My phone lit up and "Love on the Brain," by Rihanna came on. It was Alessandra's song! She was calling me!

I answered as soon as I could reach the phone.

"Alessandra," I sighed in relief, elated that she was calling me.

"I can't fucking believe you. You orchestrated this whole thing! Me in your life. God!" She was not just fuming, she was lit up with an IV of gasoline in her veins. Shit, what now?

"Explain."

"I got a call from the studio today about a contract with them, and they couldn't talk enough about how you talked them into hiring me in the first place, and how that was such a brilliant idea. How the fuck did you know who I was in order to get me that job? What did you do?"

Shit on a stick. This was something I knew could come back and bite me in the ass. I prayed it wouldn't, but of course life was like "fuck you, Joel."

"I had to see you again. I knew you were different." I sighed, with hopelessness in my breath.

"You had to see me again. So you somehow figured out who I was from the bar, and got me a job so I would be forced to be around you. Right?" When she put it like that, it sounded bad. Couldn't we think of it on a more romantic level? I went to difficult lengths to show the woman I cared about her and could be trusted. Apparently not.

"Right." Today was not going well at all.

"Goodbye, Joel." She hung up, and it was like a stab to my chest. One minute ago I was feeling good about winning back my fair maiden's heart, and now I was back to square one. No, I was further back than that. I was in the negatives. She really wouldn't want anything to do with me now that she found out I was behind getting her the job on the set.

"I can still win her back." I knocked my head against my table over and over, trying to drill the statement in.

The rest of the day was spent eating pizza and watching movies, hoping to find a trick that would work on winning Alessandra.

On my list so far:

One, humiliate yourself while singing to her, getting the marching band involved, proving you are an asshole, but will sacrifice your pride for her;

Two, take her out of the corner and dance the night away;

Three, get her a big library, because bitches love big libraries;

Four, get a bigger boat;

Five, ride up to her apartment in a white limo with roses and an umbrella, and rescue her.

There were many more after my ten-hour movie spree, but I thought those were the best. Ultimately it seemed humiliating myself would be the way to go. But that was a toughie. There would need to be some groundwork put in first; I just had to figure out where to start.

Back to the drawing board.

Chapter Thirty-Four

Alessandra

"Holy shit!" Jenson cursed from the living room, holding up two laminated cards in his hands.

"Mouth!" This kid. I walked over to look at them and saw Comic-Con passes for the whole week.

Joel.

"Can we go?" He looked at me with stars in his eyes.

I wanted to say no, because the chances of running into Joel was high and I couldn't promise that I wouldn't maim him in some way. I was running on high fury when it came to him, after finding out about him playing stalker after the bar incident to get me the job. I wasn't hired because of my skill as a makeup artist; I was hired because he wanted me to be there. They trusted him and then just happened to like my work, after the fact.

"Fine," I told Jenson, and he ran off to his room so he could tell all his friends that he was going to the highly sought-after convention.

I plopped on the couch and listened to his happiness at having those passes in his possession.

Jenson's happiness is what matters. I'd be happy another time.

Although he wasn't happy seeing me unhappy, and he thought I should talk to Joel—which I wasn't going to do—he dropped it, and was hanging closer to me, more than normal. I guessed he was either trying to comfort me or making sure I didn't curl up in a ball in the apartment.

I would be all right. I survived one asshole, and I sure as hell would survive another.

Except those memories of sleeping in Joel's arms in the hammock, or him dancing over me like a goof, would pop into my head in attempt to make me smile. And I didn't want to.

He always knew how to make me smile, to make me feel like a teenager again. Carefree, and in love.

I was still in love with him. But with time, that would fade too. At least that was my hope. I'd given the whole dating thing a try, and it didn't work out. Time to wait another thirteen years, and collect a bunch of animals. Jenson would leave me for college, and I'd become that loco lady everyone expected me to be.

Right now, it was a future that looked more appetizing than falling in love again.

The two weeks that led up to the convention were like a ticking time bomb on my schedule. I'd been hired to do contract jobs for weddings and photo shoots, and a festival booked for the fall. So things were slowly looking up for me.

I didn't need Joel Kline to get me jobs on the movie set. I had done them before, and I would keep earning my way.

Jenson and I spent the week in San Diego for the convention. He wanted to dress up as his favorite character, but because it was Joel's character he changed his mind and went for his second favorite character. I helped make his costume and did all his makeup. He looked great. I dressed up as Harley Quinn, and not the super slutty version. But I still rocked it. With my face painted up and the jester hat, plus a sea of people, Joel wouldn't find me.

But we were like magnets, always getting within range to make eye contact. He was dressed as the Joker. How fitting.

"Sexiest Harley Quinn in the building." He found me as I waited for Jenson to get his picture taken with an actor from the newest Star Wars film.

I wasn't ready for him, yet. I was still hurting, and angry. So I didn't acknowledge his existence next to me.

"I know you don't want me around, or wanna hear my words. But I'm gonna say this, and then I'll leave you alone for the rest of the week." He stepped into my view, and even all dressed up like a villain, I saw the sweet Joel in his eyes. The one that broke down my walls.

"I never cheated on you. I was upset about how hard things were for you and Jenson, so I took a walk and went to the store to get bananas. Clara, the blonde you saw online, introduced herself to me there. She wanted to see if I would be interested in helping her hospital with a big fundraiser for kids and their families. I walked her to her car, and she gave me her card. I did hug her. That was it. You are my fucking world, and I know you think it's over for us, Alessandra. But it's not. I'm not going to give up or go anywhere, until you are in my arms where you belong."

He finished what he had to say and left me standing there, taking in everything he had said but not truly processing it. Jenson was still in line, so I walked around within eyesight to distract myself from Joel's long statement. After we were finally pooped from the day, we crashed in the hotel room, and I was too tired to think over my intense encounter with Joel.

We had a different outfit everyday of the week, and beyond that first day seeing Joel, he was fairly unreachable the rest of the time. Between panels, and photo shoots, he was a busy boy. I was still in denial about what he said and decided I wouldn't think about it until I got home and had no distractions around.

Or so I thought.

Turns out I was unable to fight the fact that I was a completely crazy bitch, and ruined a relationship with someone who had been real with me, for a whole week.

Alex's words had started to suck me in like quicksand and I couldn't get out of it. He had scarred my heart so badly that I was starting to understand that I had been looking for an out with Joel. Still not believing that someone, especially an actor, would stick with me.

No wonder I had been single since Jenson had been born. I sucked at dating.

I should have believed him, and let him explain his side of things. Cooled my jets enough, but when he suggested we lay low, I panicked. I couldn't handle being left again, so I left first. Dramatically.

Now I was stuck in my thoughts, unwilling to make the first move like an adult and apologize to him. Afraid that he would fight for me to be his again. What if something happened, and he ended it? Or worse, I flipped out over something again and he couldn't take my baggage?

I rolled over in bed and searched for Joel Kline on the internet. Maybe he had done something recently that would make me hate him, and make me feel like I wasn't a bag of nuts.

And then I see it.

Him and the blonde.

With a bunch of kids and other people at a fundraiser for a children's hospital.

I shut the phone off immediately and cried.

I was an idiot.

Chapter Thirty-Five

Joel

"Aren't I supposed to be the nervous one?" My best friend stood next to me, looking sharp in his linen dress shirt, jeans, and boots. I eyed him up and down. His blond hair was like it always was, with one part falling over his blue eyes.

"You look like a hippie," I told him. This look was so beyond his normal attire, but Livia was obviously trying to dress him up for their big day.

The sun was shining down on Killian's home in the Keys, and in a few moments he would marry the love of his life.

"You said she showed up yesterday?" I asked, not so subtly. He shook his head and ignored me.

Music started playing, and the few people that were in attendance stood for the bride and her crew.

The wedding was held in the back yard of Killian's cottage on the water. They had set up a bamboo arch with linen hanging on each end. Rose petals were scattered to make an aisle in the middle, with maybe fifteen people total watching as Livia's mother came into view in a beautiful lavender dress. She was Livia's only bridesmaid, since I was Killian's only best man. His Salt and Pepper father-like figure, Lucas Lonsello, was initially going to be the best man, but he ended up being our clergyman instead. One of his many talents, it seemed.

Livia's mom gave me a wink as she passed in front of me and took her place opposite of us. She was nonstop chatting with me in the car when she picked me up from the airport. I was very thankful when we pulled up to Killian's house, so I could get a break from her complimenting me and talking about how my abs looked in my costume.

I know everyone watched the bride as she came walking down the aisle on her father's arm, but I made sure to look at my friend as he followed his bride's every movement. His eyes were so intense, like nothing I had ever seen. It was a look that said so much, without the need for words. He was watching his world walk toward him.

She did look beautiful, in a thin-strapped dress that was cut low in the front then blossomed out to her bare feet.

Her long blond hair was loose, and a wreath of flowers circled her head. Her eyes were on Killian's, with a big smile on her face.

When her father kissed her cheek gently and handed her off to Killian to start the ceremony, he pulled her in and did not hold back pressing his lips to hers.

Everyone laughed, and then I heard a familiar tone. My head whipped around, and I finally found her.

My goddess of the sea was standing in a wine-colored dress that wrapped around her waist then flared out to her knees. She had sandals on that accentuated her tan and toned calves. When my eyes travelled back up to her face, she had her eyes on the couple who were finally breaking up their liplock session to actually get married.

She was radiant.

I'd been so busy with the convention and meetings that I hadn't gotten the chance to continue my endeavor in trying to win her back, but I had time, and I wasn't giving up.

Even though I could tell she was trying to ignore me, our eyes met, and it gave me hope.

I gave her a wink and then turned back toward the happy couple.

"Livia and Killian have each written their own vows." Lucas smiled and gestured to Killian to start his. I had asked him what he was going to say, and he had only shrugged, so I was very attentive now. What would a man who didn't speak his feelings much choose to say to his bride as a vow to show his promise of forever?

"'Say You Won't Let Go,' by James Arthur." He smiled at Livia, and she burst into happy tears. Hell, even *my* eyes started to water at his theme song choice. It was so perfect for them, and it was everything they deserved.

"Seriously." She wiped away her tears and looked at Lucas. I handed Killian her simple, white gold ring and slid my hands back in my pockets.

"How am I not supposed to kiss him after that?" she asked as Killian slid her band on her finger.

"Two more minutes. Patience, Fille précieuse," Lucas teased her in French and then told her it was her turn.

"'Stay With You,' by John Legend." She wiped more of her tears, and her mother handed her Killian's black band. She slid the metal over his tanned finger, shaking from the happiness that was radiating from her in waves.

Lucas could barely get the words out before they were wrapped in each other's arms and sealing their vows with a kiss.

Their story was full of rain and sunshine, but they danced in the showers together and found happiness in the moment.

Everyone erupted in a series of laughter, hooting, and clapping.

Together they walked down the aisle as Mr. And Mrs. Lemarque, and I found myself watching them with excitement. They were going to live a great life together.

I also couldn't wait until I talked Alessandra into marrying me. I would probably be dragging her by her cute, pedicured toes to the altar, but I already Spartan-kicked her into love, so it was just our style.

Speaking of Alessandra…

I moved quickly after the couple and stopped in front of her. Jenson was standing next to her, and I said hey. He gave me a quick head jerk but stayed quiet, ever loyal to his mother.

"Let's give them today without us ruining it, all right? We can talk tomorrow." She held out her hand in a truce, and even though it's not what I wanted, she had a point. I didn't know how talking to Alessandra about our future was going to go. She could start throwing things at me or we could end up screwing on the grass.

So I shook her hand and leaned in close.

"But I'm still going to dance with you tonight." I left her with that and helped the couple get into his truck so they could head to the little reception site.

Everyone cleared out and followed behind them, but mysteriously, the newlyweds were the last people to get to the party.

Livia was blushing, and her hair was more on the messy side, when they finally walked in together, hand-in-hand. Guess they pulled off somewhere and put that bunk to good use, consummating the marriage.

They jumped right into their first dance on the tiled floor to a song about taking a long drive.

A song that meant so much to them, apparently.

It was cute.

Then we all ate our food and the party officially began.

Chapter Thirty-Six

Joel

Alessandra was dancing with Jenson when I decided it was time to make my move, praying the kid wouldn't let me down.

"Mind if I cut in?" I bowed, playing it up, which made the kid smile. His mother was giving him the stink-eye, but like every teenager, he liked to rebel now and then.

He placed her hand in mine and walked off.

You could see the steam coming out of her ears, that her son just kinda threw her at me. Good to know he was still willing to give me a shot.

"Dance with me, Alessandra; let's not ruin the happy couple's special day." I pulled her in and placed our joined hands over my heart. She let me lead, and I began to move us as a new song came on. The perfect slow melody about finding the perfect woman, and never giving her up.

We glided in our little square in silence, but not in anger. She was in that moment with me, feeling our bodies as we moved in sync, something we never had a problem with.

The lyrics were hitting me so hard that I leaned down to whisper the words in her ear.

"I can't do this." She ripped her hand out from mine and fled the dance floor.

Not this time, love. I followed behind her with grace, so no one would know I was in pursuit. She entered the bathroom, and I didn't even think twice about going in there to get her.

"Let me in, Alessandra." I knocked on the stall door, and unlike the last time we were in this situation, she didn't open for me.

I bent down and made sure there was no one in the other stalls before doing something crazy. I crawled under the door.

"What the hell is wrong with you?" she snapped and backed as far away from me as she could get.

"I'm willing to do anything," I told her as I stood, brushing my shirt and jeans off.

"You're crazy." She shook her head, and I could tell that her eyes were starting to water with tears.

"Crazy for you." I was a cheese ball, and she called me out on it. But I didn't let that deter me; I walked over to her and looked her in the eyes. She looked like a frightened animal, but what was she afraid of?

I leaned in and kissed her gently, trying to express all of my words through touch. She let out a strangled cry, then wrapped her arms around me and met my passion with her own brand.

"I'm sorry; I don't think I can do this again." She broke away from the kiss and whispered her rejection between us. I ignored it.

"We'll take it slow." For as long as she needed.

"I just can't. I'm sorry I overreacted. I just—" She pulled back and ran for the door.

"Just not right now." She looked back at me and then exited the bathroom.

Well, that didn't go how I wanted. I mean, I saw it in her eyes that she still loved me, and wanted me. But something was holding her back.

I left the bathroom with two goals in my mind: putting my acting skills to work for the rest of the night so Killian and Livia wouldn't know there was anything going on with me, and then hitting a bottle of something hard.

We sent the couple off for their hotel room in a painted and ribbon-decorated truck. Their flight to Australia departed tomorrow for their month-long honeymoon.

As soon as everyone left, I made eye contact with Alessandra briefly before turning back inside to grab whatever bottle I could get before heading back to my hotel room.

I woke up with my music blasting from my plugged-in phone.

My head was pounding, and I needed something to wash the nasty, rancid taste out of my mouth. Ignoring the music, I crawled to the shower and shed my clothing in the water's spray, not caring what mess I was making.

How did yesterday go so wrong for me?

That was pretty much the question that kept going on and on in my head, with every sip of my drink.

I washed the smell of alcohol off me, and tried to find some food in the room to help my sour stomach. I found a cookie on the dresser that I got when checking in to the hotel two days ago. It would work until I called up room service for something with more nutrition.

My body fell back against the bed as I ate, and I tried not to think about anything besides having faith.

This was the part of the movie where the hero thinks all hope is lost, but then something happens—an epiphany if you will— giving him the strength and the knowledge of what he has to do to come to victory.

I just needed my side character, or something to give me a clue as to what I should do.

An hour I waited for my stomach to settle, and the universe to provide me with the answers, and when a song by the world's top pop star came on, I officially knew I was screwed. This hero wasn't getting the girl.

Until I listened to the song, and ignored who sang it.

This song literally had my salvation.

Never in my life would I think Taylor Swift would be the one to tell me how to get the girl.

But here I was, the hero who knew what he had to do.

She was the Alessandra to my Joel, period buddies for life.

Chapter Thirty-Seven

Alessandra

"Okay, lift your arm there, please," I asked the older woman, trying to get my airbrush at a better angle to spray the side of her very droopy breast.

"All done! You guys look great." I smiled and took the cash from the white-haired woman who was currently standing naked in front of me with only the body paint I had just covered her with. All three of them were naked, actually, but they had matching breasts that looked like dogs and their floppy ears.

I stashed my money in my bag and waited for my next person to show me what they wanted.

It had been two months since the wedding, and I was currently back in the Keys and painting half-naked and naked people for Fantasy Fest. It was like Mardi Gras, but way less clothing.

Some of the costumes were pretty awesome, and even the body painting was on point. It was something I liked doing on the side, because I got to really show my artistic abilities. Plus, I always made a ton of cash doing this festival. Skilled painters that could make people look like they were wearing clothes when they weren't are like gold here. I had practiced for years to get to this point, and I flaunted it. I was wearing pasties and bikini-style panties, and made myself look like I was wearing a cropped shirt and shorts. I'd gotten so many compliments and people wanting to take my picture.

It was the final night, and the parade was going to be starting soon. Everyone was nicely buzzed or downright intoxicated and ready for the party to kick off.

I always enjoyed the parade. People were very creative, and it was nice to see the winners of each category. I've heard there were going to be some good ones this year.

A man with jet-black hair walked by in tight boxers that had been painted over as part of his full-body Superman getup. His swagger held familiarity in my head, but that was silly. Joel wasn't here. He said he wasn't giving up on me, but that was a lie. I pushed him too far, and he wasn't coming for me. Especially not here.

I finished working on my last client for the night and closed up my little tent so I could watch the parade.

Music was on full blast, and the cars and floats started coming down the road.

It was fun to see everyone dancing and having a blast. My favorite float was the Lucille Ball one. They were all dressed in different Lucy outfits and acting out her personality. It was hilarious to watch. Confetti was floating in the sky from the two men on a wedding cake float that passed before, and it gave the whole festival a magical feeling, like anything could happen tonight.

All of a sudden, the whole strip of Duvall Street went black.

I looked around, and everyone was just as surprised as I was.

Only the floats were lit up, except the one in front of my section of the street. It was dark, and there were murmurs about something happening. Maybe too much partying had finally happened in Key West.

Then a voice came through a speaker.

Singing the beginning words to "Can't Take My Eyes off You."

"You're just too good to be true."

A male voice.

Then a spotlight from one of the balconies hit the dark float, showing the singer by himself, standing in full Superman body paint with jet black hair.

Joel.

"Oh my God." My eyes widened and then the crowd jumped with me, as the whole strip lit up and a marching band that came out of nowhere began playing the song on their instruments.

My face was red as he danced and sang straight to me. The crowd noticed who he was pointing to and parted like the Red Sea so he could serenade me with his merry band.

This was so embarrassing.

And sweet.

And dammit, he didn't give up on me.

Tears started to coat my sight, and I laughed at his theatrics.

If there was one thing Joel could do better than anyone, it was put on a show, and humiliate himself for all to see.

But he was doing it for me.

He jumped down each step when the cymbals banged together and then walked over to me, singing his heart out. He wasn't the best singer in the world, but I didn't care.

He took the scene straight from *10 Things I Hate About You*, and if Kat Stratford the man-hater could give Heath Ledger's character a chance after this performance, then I could take another chance on love with Joel.

He stood in front of me and rang out the final word, holding his arms out for me to accept him.

I didn't just do that—I jumped straight onto him, wrapping my legs around his waist, kissing him for every day I missed him, wasting so much time being scared.

"I love you, crazy man," I told him and ignored the crowd as they celebrated the hero getting his girl.

With me in his arms, he carried me back to his '90s themed float and set me in a chair.

"I'm never giving up, Lips, and I want you for worse or for better. I want you forever and ever." He got down on one knee and pulled out a ring from a little pouch from his briefs.

"I'm not touching that thing if it's been hanging out with your sweaty balls," I teased, but held my hand out. Of course, I'd marry this man.

He slid the big diamond solitaire on my finger, with an even bigger smile on his face.

I reached over and pulled him in with my newly blinged-out finger and pressed my smile to his.

Music started playing over the speakers of his float, and I couldn't help but laugh.

"The girl told me how to get the girl; I figured it was our end of the story credits song."

My crazy man.

We kissed and celebrated our love to the tune of a Taylor Swift song.

Epilogue

Two months later

Joel

"Are you sure this is going to work?" Jenson asked, looking scared at what we were about to do.

"It's easy. You were the mastermind of this mission. You ready, kid?" I put my hand over his shoulder to help calm his nerves. I remember jumping out of an airplane for the first time.

"Okay, let's go." I looked behind him at my best man, and he gave me the nod. Jenson was riding tandem with Killian for the flight down. Both of us were very experienced with sky diving, certificates and all. Whether wrong of not, I used my movie star status and an extra tip to waiver the minor form for Jenson.

We both jumped and then we were flying through the sky as our dramatic entrance to our big day. As we soared through the sky, I thought about what Alessandra was going to look like down there as my bride.

Jenson wanted an action wedding, and we didn't give a shit how we got married, so we let him plan it.

The men were skydiving out of a plane as our entrance, and Alessandra would be driven in by my T-REX three wheeler by her father.

Then we would be married by Lucas, since Jenson thought he was cool. That was all he wanted, but I had a few other plans to make it a special day for all of us. One in particular I thought was going to knock my bride's garters off.

The ground was coming in quick, and we released our parachutes with perfect timing. The crowd below us was small, mostly our close friends and family. My siblings and their little stinkers were waving at us as we came to a halt on the group by Lucas.

Perfect.

I looked at Killian and held my hand out for a high-five to him and then Jenson. We nailed it. Everyone cheered and then I heard tires burning rubber behind the crowd.

I guess Alessandra's dad decided to have some fun with the three-wheeler before dropping her off. Or he was trying to make her entrance dramatic, too.

We were a big bag of loco. But I wouldn't have it any other way. Some people loved the intense, all-consuming love that made you wanna cry every time you saw your love.

We were more of a laugh, goof around, and smile kind of couple. Fun love.

Alessandra was escorted by her father out of the three-wheeler and she walked down the aisle, a vision in off-white.

Couldn't lie with color and say she was a virgin. That ship sailed a long time ago.

Her hair was curled in that classic pinup wave I liked, with red lips that were ready for some kissing.

Every curve of her body was covered in lace and tulle, with off-the-shoulder straps so I could bite her shoulders with ease tonight, and a high slit that gave easy access up her dress.

She smiled at me like she knew what I was thinking. I was thinking about how I was going to call her my wife over and over tonight, just before making her come on my cock.

Her dad kissed her cheek and handed her over to me. Jenson stood beside me, looking at his mom with a goofy, teenaged grin.

I didn't pull her in for a kiss like my best friend did with his bride; I had a better plan.

Lucas was informed of my plan and started the ceremony like any other, saying why we were all gathered here today, and then handed the mic over to me.

Alessandra looked at me like *why the hell was I deviating from what we practiced,* but this wasn't at the rehearsal last night.

"Thanks, guys, for coming out for our crazy wedding. It means so much to me that you are here today. Not only do I get to marry this crazy bitch, but you will also get to witness a very key start to our new life." I smiled and let go of Alessandra's hands before turning to Jenson.

"You're the coolest kid I know, and I know I'm about to marry your mom, but I needed to ask you a question first. Okay?" He was looking around like he didn't know what he was supposed to do, so he just nodded.

"I don't wanna be your stepdad, Jenson." I told him and his eyes got wide and his face fell a little.

"I wanna be your real dad. Will you let me adopt you as mine, and be a crazy Kline, too?" The smile on his face was so wide I thought it was going to split in two.

"Fuck yeah!" he answered and then I pulled him in for a hug.

"I love you, kid," I told him, and he started crying. When I turned back around to truly make my family complete, tears were falling down Alessandra's cheeks, coasting over her bright smile, and falling onto the ground.

Lucas continued the vows, and when it was time to kiss my girl, I grabbed her by the hand and spun her out then back in, and dipped her down, kissing her movie-star style.

She started laughing when "The Man" by Aloe Blacc started playing from speakers that had been set up behind the crowd and shook her head.

"Seriously?"

"Seriously." I Spartan-kicked my girl into love and then I tamed her lioness soul. I was *the fucking man*.

I pulled her back up to a standing position and then grabbed the bag that Killian gave me.

"Okay, people. We have ten minutes to get from this location to the reception. Zombies are coming, and you have two minutes to get your gun and prepare yourselves. When they come, we shoot and run to the safety of the pavilion." I grabbed a Nerf gun from the bag and cocked it.

Alessandra looked at me like I lost my damn mind, but then reached down and grabbed a gun.

Jenson grabbed his gun, and together as a family we battled the zombies and made it to safety, where I kissed my wife through the night and took my sweet time giving her fun love back at our hotel suite.

Our love was crazy.

But that's how I got the girl.

The End

*Keep reading for the first chapter of Long Drive.

Killian and Livia's story.

*To stay up to date on ALL things Jessica Florence

Sign up for my Epic Newsletter!!

Thank you all for taking a chance on my stories <3

Playlist

Cowboy Casanova- Carrie Underwood

Maneater- Nelly Furtado

Classic-MKTO

On My Mind- Ellie Goulding

Teenage Dream- Katy Perry

Shape Of You- Ed Sheeran

It's Gonna Be meme - 'NSYNC

Dangerous Woman- Ariana Grande

Makin'Good Love-Avant

The Man- Aloe Blacc

Can't Help Falling In Love- Elvis Presley

Dive- Ed Sheeran

Bad Things- Machine Gun Kelly ft. Camila Cabello

Take a Bow- Rihanna ft. Ne-Yo

Say You Won't Let Go- James Arthur

Perfect- Ed Sheeran

Love on the Brain- Rihanna

How You Get The Girl- Taylor swift

Can't Take My Eyes Off of You- 10 Things I Hate About You soundtrack

Chapter One

Livia

"I'll give you ten thousand dollars to let me ride around with you for a month." The man with the hood over his head froze while drinking his coffee, and turned slowly to look at me.

Holy hell, he was more attractive than I thought. He had blue eyes mixed with gray, kind of like the ocean after a storm. Murky, but calm. It was my favorite time to sit by the water, as it smoothed out to look like glass. Well, used to be my favorite time.

"I think you have the wrong guy." His voice was deep, and matched the after-storm effect of his eyes. He pushed his medium-length golden blond hair away from his eyes, which was a failed attempt, since it went right back to where it was.

"The other drivers said you were the only one that is driving out of state. I need to get out of Florida." His eyebrows drew in together, and looked at the group of men sitting at a table. They were the ones I'd talked to. Some people would think I was crazy, and right now I was probably a little loony, but who was I trying to impress? No one. Not even this attractive truck driver. His eyes took me in and then got stuck on my eyes. Yeah, I know, freak show eyes. I was always picked on as a kid for having different color eyes. My right one was blue, and my left one was light green with brown splashed in it. I've heard all the jokes before. His eyes held mine briefly before answering.

"No." He turned to finish drinking his coffee. No? *NO?* That just wasn't going to work for me. My car had just broken down, and it would be a few more days before it was fixed. I didn't want to wait. I needed to get out and do something. My life was in ruins, and I couldn't stay still. I needed to be on the road. What better way to do that, than with someone who was on the road all the time?

"Fifteen thousand. I'll give you half now, and at the end of the month I'll give you the other half. As long as I'm not lying in a ditch somewhere. So no killing or raping me," I somewhat joked with him. I really didn't need any more horrible experiences. I'd gone through enough in the past couple months to last me for a while. He turned back towards me and just stared at my face, trying to figure me out.

"I know this all seems crazy, but I just need to get away. I feel like this is what I need. I swear I'm not a loon. Please don't say no," I begged, hoping my pure desperation would come through, and he would say yes to my outlandish proposal. His head turned slightly to the side, and that long piece of hair blocked part of his right eye, blocking me from seeing any emotion that it held. Unsure if he believed me or not, he simply turned back towards his coffee. Then he huffed.

"Sure."

That was a yes! Holy shit, this plan worked! I was going on a month-long road trip with a strange, attractive, trucker! This was exactly what I needed.

"Great! I'll go grab my small suitcase and get rid of my car real quick. I'll be right back." I turned and walked away quickly before he could change his mind. As soon as I opened the door, the Florida air hit me. It was nice out, being January, but I was ready for a change. The little mechanic's shop was attached to the truck stop I was just inside, which was convenient.

"Hello!" I called out to the mechanic that was working on my car.

"Hey! I just got off the phone; your transmission will be here in two days." He smiled at me while wiping a big glob of grease on his forehead in an attempt to wipe the sweat off his face. I shook my head.

"That's okay. I actually have a different plan of action now. Wanna buy my car?" The guy just laughed and went to work back on my car. What was with people not believing me today?

"I'm serious. I don't want it anymore." I walked over to him and stood close. Crossing my arms across my chest.

"Uh, this is a really nice car. Don't think you want to just get rid of it." This was starting to get frustrating.

"I know. I'm just moving on with my life, and this was the car my ex-fiancé gave me as a Christmas gift. I don't even really like it. Not my style." And that was the truth. I didn't care for flashy or expensive cars. When Lane surprised me with this new BMW SUV, I faked enthusiasm as best as I could. And sadly, he thought it was real. I was raised in the country; my dad had a beat-up old truck, and Mom drove a Jeep. I figured he had known I wouldn't have cared for it, but he got it for me anyways.

"Oh, uh. What do you want for it?" He rubbed more grease on his head. I felt compelled to tell him he was doing that, and opened my mouth right when a little kid ran through the garage.
"Daddy!" The kid was probably around five. He looked like his dad, with curly brown hair, and tan skin. He even had a little grease on his hands, as if he was trying to be like his dad. The mechanic, whose coverall said *Joe,* picked up the kid for a hug then set him back down.

My chest began to ache, seeing them together. You could tell they really loved each other. I felt the stinging of tears threaten my eyes, and I made a quick decision. I opened the door and climbed in to grab the papers out of the glove box. I wasn't sure why I had grabbed them in the first place for this trip, but now I was glad I did. After finding a pen in there, too, I signed the paper, and climbed back out of the SUV.

"Here, it's yours." I handed him the title to the car. I didn't need the money, and I didn't want to deal with the car anymore. Joe's mouth dropped open, and he held out his hands.

"Are you serious?" He was in shock. His son was just looking at me with an uncertain grin on his face. Yeah, this was totally worth it. They would have a nice family car to drive around in.

"Yep. Have fun!" I grabbed my suitcase out of the back seat and walked back towards the little diner on the other end of the truck stop. The man I made a deal with was standing next to a big, blue semi-trailer truck, stretching. He was taller than I had thought, and bigger, too. As I neared the truck, I finally took him in. The low-lit diner hadn't done him justice. He wasn't attractive; he was beautiful. His hair was hanging down as he bent to touch his toes. When he lifted up and stretched his arms over his head, his blue thermal shirt rode up, and I could see tan skin—muscular tan skin. His jeans rode low and covered brown boots.

The clicking of my own girly version of trucker boots alerted him to my approach.

"Hiya!" I waved with my free hand. He dropped his hands and waited for me to get closer.

"We're driving by my rules, none of that peeing-every-hour shit, okay?" I just nodded. I had peed before I talked to him; I would be good for a little while.

"Where are we heading?" My excitement for this trip was hard to contain, but I didn't wanna weird him out with my exuberance.

"Orlando," he huffed. He was certainly not a big talker. That's all right. I could be quiet for a little while. Then I could probably talk for the both of us.

"Then where?"

"California." Heck, yeah!

"All right! Shall we get this show on the road?" I was so ready to get started. This was a new chapter in my life. I had no clue where my storyline was going to head, but I was willing to turn the pages one by one to find out.

He didn't answer me, but opened his door and climbed in. So, not the gentleman type. That's okay. I was a big girl. I looked back at the truck stop one last time. Was I really going to do this? Take off with a stranger and travel across the country with him?

"Yes. Yes, you are, Livia," I told myself, and strode off towards my new home for the next month. This was going to be something—whether it was a good something or a bad something remained to be seen.

More Books by Jessica Florence

The Final KO

I fight bitches for a living.

Which makes finding a decent guy hard when you're a female MMA fighter. None of them have been my equal. I yearn for a man who can push me to reach new heights and challenge me. A man who will treat me like a lady then lift me up by my ass and impale me against the wall.

But when Arson Kade, MMA's top fighter and notorious manwhore, declares he's that man for me I have my doubts. Any sane woman would.

There seems to be more to Arson than the rumors that surround him, but will it make me fall hard or run for the hills? I know I've got no choice but to hold on for the ride.

It's the main event and my heart's on the line.
But will it be the Final KO?

The Final Chase

I never thought a wallaby, Henley shirts, and a horse's rectal exam would have anything in common.
Turns out they did.
Jake Wild. Owner of Wild Rescue for exotic animals.
He's everything I'm not, my polar opposite.
I'm heels and my salon,
he's dirt and his creatures.
But much like the animals he cares for, he's got that carnal edge.
He's the type of man you crawl on your hands and knees for with your ass up in the air.
He bites, he's on the hunt, and now I'm his prey.
A chance meeting and a bet started the undeniable attraction between us.
But I'm not giving my heart and soul away that easy, he's going to have to catch me first.
It's the ultimate game of cat and mouse.
But will it be the Final Chase?

Guiding Lights

He sings of suffering. His eyes hold the pain of living in sorrow.
The moment our gaze meets recognition flares within.
We are tortured souls drifting in a sea of darkness.
He knows I have secrets that I'll never tell.
I am numb.
I am broken.
I am dirty.
I can never be the guiding light through the darkness he thinks I am.
I have forsaken my past, I rely on keeping myself shut off.
But he has secrets too, secrets that would destroy everything I have left.
I wish things were different, that maybe we could be each other's lifeline.
But destiny drags us down like an anchor.
The broken can only drift in the sea barely staying afloat.

Blinding Lights

She dances with a passion I'll never know.
Seeing her again tears me at the seams.
She was never mine.
My soul is stained with the darkness of death.
I have killed.
I have tortured.
I have lost.
Her soul is too bright for the shadows within,
and her determination to be the flame in my heart could kill us both.
Still, I want her, I crave her.
But not even her blinding lights can fight away the darkness threatening us both.
Eventually, everything gets snuffed out.

Weighing of the Heart

What happens when the myths of old become reality?

Thalia Alexander has lived her life in peace until her twenty-fifth birthday when she has a strange dream about a man.

A tall, dark, and sexy man that shows up at her work the next morning.

Tristan Jacks is trouble with a capital T, but for some strange reason she is drawn to him like nothing she has ever experienced before. He has this possessiveness and adoration for her that she can't explain. It's like they have known each other forever.

Thalia's strange dreams continue to stalk her as her relationship with Tristan builds to be a love that will last the ages.

And when those dreams and reality start to clash, will Thalia be able to handle the truth?

Could the world of ancient myths truly exist in modern times?

Evergreen

It was supposed to be an easy stake out.
Until a bunch of bachelorettes mobbed me, changing my life forever.

I couldn't get Andi Slaton, with her red hair, blue eyes, and cotton candy flavored lip gloss out of my head.

But when she offers herself to aid the FBI to help me take down the biggest criminal family in Tampa, Florida, my very sanity is put to the test watching her spend time with my arch enemy.

She's everything I want, I will be everything to her.
We will be Evergreen.

About the Author

Jessica Florence,
Writer of Alpha Males & Fairy Tales
Author <3 PotterHead <3 Movie Geek Extraordinaire.

When she's not writing her next invigorating story. You can find her running her own business, and spending time with her husband and daughter in southwest Florida.
Jessica loves to interact with her readers, find her on

https://www.facebook.com/JessicaFlorenceAuthor
Www.JessicaFlorenceAuthor.com
JessicaFlorenceAuthor@gmail.com
https://twitter.com/florence_jess

Acknowledgements

In no particular order.

I want to thank my fairies. For being awesome and keeping me going with your excitement.

Marissa, M.A. Scott, & Dayna. You guys rock my socks and I am soo thankful for you guys and your help with this book.

Kiezha, you turn my mess into something readable ;) I can never thank you enough for it.

Judy, thank you for your extra set of eyes. I am very happy I found you.

Sarah, girl, you are the cover goddess, and will be stuck with me forever. Your work is beautiful and you brought Joel to life.

Erin, my homeslice. Thank you for all the work you have done for me and my releases!

Hubs, thank you for our fun love. It really inspired a lot of this story. Your support means the world to me.

Baby, keep being cute.

I appreciate all of the blogs that have helped me to get to this part and have taken the time to read this book or that have supported me in any way. You guys are the mac to my cheese.

Readers, book friends, bloggers, and author friends. I love you bitches. You guys are the best and I can't imagine a world without you.

You've all taken a chance on me in some way and I love you all to death.

Made in the USA
Columbia, SC
19 July 2023